MORE PRAISE FOR

the Other BOY

"Shane's story presents a range of experiences of how people react to someone who is transgender. More importantly, his story walks readers through what it feels like to know your body doesn't align with your gender. Shane is positioned just right to surface the problems that come with negotiating friends and romance as an ordinary boy."

—*The Bulletin of the Center for Children's Books*

"This book is a must for public library collections."

—ALA's GLBT Reviews

"I loved this book. I'm tempted to start reading it again right now rather than start a new book."

—YA Books Central

"I love the honest portrayal of a transitioning transgender middle school boy struggling with when and how to share his true self with his friends. Very well written, yet accessible to a wide range of kids."

—Youth Services Book Review

the Other Boy

M. G. HENNESSEY

Illustrated by SFÉ R. MONSTER

HARPER
An Imprint of HarperCollinsPublishers

The Other Boy

Text copyright © 2016 by M. G. Hennessey

Illustrations copyright © 2016 by Sfé R. Monster

ISBN 978-0-06-242767-0

Typography by Michelle Gengaro-Kokmen
19 20 21 22 23   PC/BRR   10 9 8 7 6 5 4 3 2

❖

First paperback edition, 2019

*For all the transgender
and gender-expansive children,
and for everyone
who loves them unconditionally*

ONE

"Dude, you're kidding, right?" Josh threw the baseball up with one hand, then deftly snatched it out of the air with the other.

"Sorry, man." I shrugged. "I've got to go."

"But it's the last game. If we lose, we won't make regionals." Josh tossed me the ball.

I caught it and spun it in my hand. The ball felt natural there, like it belonged; that's what I loved about baseball, it always felt right. "So win without me."

Josh scowled. "Who's gonna pitch? Dylan? He sucks."

"Nah, he's okay," I said, even though Dylan threw two balls for every strike.

Josh scuffed his shoes along the sidewalk as we kept walking. It was already ninety degrees, way too hot for April.

"I can't believe your mom is making you miss the game for a stupid trip." Josh shook his head. "She's usually so cool."

"Yeah," I agreed, feeling a twinge of guilt. I hated to miss such an important game, but I didn't really have a choice. And I couldn't even tell Josh why. He'd been my best friend since we moved to L.A. three years ago. But sometimes, lying was just easier on everybody.

Josh started to step off the curb, but Maria the crossing guard snapped, "Wait until I say okay!"

"There aren't even any cars coming," he grumbled.

"Maybe they're invisible," I offered, and Josh cracked up.

Scowling, Maria marched into the middle of the road, brandishing her sign like it was a sword as she waved us across.

"So we can go now?" Josh said. "Are you sure?"

"Don't be jerks," said a familiar voice behind us.

I flushed bright red as Madeline Duncan stepped off the curb. She threw Maria a radiant smile and said, "*Buenos días, Señora Vasquez.*"

Maria beamed back at her. "*Buenos días, Madeline.*"

"Suck-up," Josh muttered as we followed.

I didn't answer, fixated on how Madeline's long red hair swished back and forth across her backpack as she walked. She was holding the straps, which made her elbows jut out behind her. Today she was wearing a pink skirt, bright orange leggings, and blue Converse high-tops.

"Did you catch the game last night? Giants are looking good this season, bro," Josh said.

"Yeah, great," I muttered, distracted. Did Madeline really think I was a jerk? I wanted to catch up and explain that we were just messing around, but then Josh would tease me about caring what Madeline thought.

I did care, though. A lot.

Just last year, a whole group of us would spend recess running around after each other playing tag. It didn't really matter if you were a girl or a boy, because everyone was just friends. But in sixth grade that stopped, as if an agreement had been struck without anyone ever saying anything. Now the girls hung out on the benches by the swings while the boys shot hoops.

I liked basketball okay, but there were days when I really missed tag.

"What's with you?" Josh asked, tossing me the ball again.

"Nothing," I mumbled. Madeline had stopped to talk to a couple of her friends. She said something, and they all laughed.

He followed my gaze and raised an eyebrow. "Ooh. You like her?"

"No!" I protested, but it was too late.

Josh smirked and chanted, "Shane likes Maddie . . . Shane likes Maddie."

I elbowed him in the ribs. "Shut up!"

"Ow." He gave me a wounded look. "Chill, dude."

"You chill," I muttered back. Everyone was hustling to get through the door before the bell rang. Someone bumped me hard from behind, nearly knocking me down. I caught myself and spun around to find Nico Palmer sneering at me. He was a big kid who played for a different club team, the Mustangs; they'd gone to regionals the past five years, so they were kind of a dynasty. "Watch it!"

"Move it, loser," he said as he shoved through the next knot of kids on the stairs. "Cardinals suck."

"Mustangs suck worse!" Josh called after him.

"Just ignore him," I said. "He's an idiot."

"Yeah, but a good hitter. You think we'll end up playing them?"

I shrugged. "If we win." Unlike our team, the Mustangs were pretty much guaranteed a spot at regionals.

"Maybe they'll choke," Josh said hopefully, tucking the baseball into the side pocket of his backpack. "See you in math?"

"Yeah, see you." I couldn't help it, my eyes were still locked on Madeline halfway up the stairs.

I pushed through the bottleneck and finally made it

to my locker at the end of the hall. It was still so cool to have a real locker; last year, we'd hung our backpacks on pegs outside class. This felt more grown-up, like they were finally trusting us with something.

Decorating the locker was a big deal, too. I had pictures of my favorite players taped inside; all Giants, of course. Los Angeles was Dodgers country, but Mom and I had lived in San Francisco through third grade, so technically they're my hometown team. Plus their colors are orange and black, which remind me of Halloween, which also just happens to be my favorite holiday. I mean, dressing up as whatever you want *and* getting free candy? It doesn't get more awesome than that.

I took out the books for my first few classes, then hurried to homeroom. It was the only class I shared with Madeline, since she was in the gifted program, which kind of made me wish I was better at school.

The room was half empty, and Madeline was in her usual seat by the window. Sometimes, if the window was open, a breeze would send the smell of her hair over, and for ten whole minutes I was breathing in strawberry bubble gum.

I stopped and scanned the chairs, like I was trying to decide which one to take. In case anyone was paying attention, I gave a little shrug and slouched over to the one next to her. I pulled out my sketchbook to work on the drawing I'd started last night.

"That's pretty good."

I looked up. Madeline was smiling at me, her lips shiny with gloss. "Thanks."

"What is it?" she asked, leaning over and scrunching up her face.

I turned the notebook toward her. "It's an alien."

"Cool," she said.

I wondered if she really thought so; suddenly the drawing seemed kind of dumb. Before I could explain that I was working on a graphic novel about a space explorer, Mr. Peters came in and boomed, "Seats, please!"

The rest of the kids grumbled and scraped chairs as they took their desks.

Madeline leaned over and whispered, "Big game this weekend, right?"

"Huh?"

"Olive's brother is on your team," she said with a smile. "He said you really need to win."

"Um, yeah." The fact that she even knew I played got me flustered. "But I have to go out of town with my mom." I felt a twinge of embarrassment. In sixth grade, admitting you had parents was mortifying, even though we obviously all did.

"Bummer," she said, making a face. "I'm sleeping

over at Olive's, so I was going to check it out. Where are you going?"

"San Francisco," I explained. "My dad still lives there."

"How cool! I've never been." Madeline gave a little sigh. "What's it like?"

I struggled for words to describe how it was colder, and foggier, but a lot prettier. The way that the Golden Gate Bridge looked like it was reaching out to embrace you when you crossed it, and how if you hit it at the right time of day, the sunset made the water glow like gold. But Mr. Peters started calling roll before I could answer.

The bell rang, and everyone started talking again. Over the din, Madeline said, "Have a good trip!"

"Thanks." As we walked out together, I tried to come up with something clever and charming that would make her laugh, but my mind was blank. Kaitlyn and Olive were suddenly flanking her, talking fast and giggling, and Madeline walked away with them.

At lunch that day, Josh plunked his backpack on the bench and announced, "I've got it!"

I was gulping down my sandwich, keeping an eye on the basketball courts. In Los Angeles, the weather was almost always nice enough to eat outside. There was an unspoken competition between the boys to claim the bench closest to the ball bins. Whoever finished first got the best basketballs, the ones that weren't half flat. Dylan was one bench over, already halfway through his lunch. Keeping an eye on him, I asked, "Got what?"

"Sleep over at my place this weekend!" Josh said, spreading his arms wide. "Then you won't miss the game."

"Can't," I said through a mouthful of sandwich.

"Why not?"

"Two nights is a lot," I said, swigging some water. "I don't think your mom will go for that."

"Are you kidding? I swear, she likes you better than me." Josh mimicked her, adopting a high, singsong voice. "That Shane is such a nice boy. Did you see how he held the door? Why don't you have manners like that?"

I shoved him. He shoved me back, almost knocking me off the bench. I couldn't help but think that a year ago, I was stronger than him.

"Anyway, I'm gonna ask her."

"It won't matter." I dug through my reusable lunch sack: there was an apple, a vegan cookie, and tofu jerky. I could save all that for later; the sandwich would be enough for now.

"Why not?"

"Because"—I shrugged—"I haven't seen my dad in a while."

Josh gaped at me in disbelief. "Um, hello? If we lose, that's it. No regionals. Just tell him you'll come when baseball is over."

I shook my head. "He's made big plans. I can't bail on him."

"Like what?" Josh demanded.

"I don't know. Plans." I balled up my wax-paper bag and threw it at the trash can ten feet away; it cleared the rim. "Boom!"

"You know how mad everyone will be if we lose?"

"You won't."

"We might."

"Then we'll win next season," I said, even though the thought of coming so close and then not making it was truly awful. If the Cardinals did lose, I'd be kicking myself for not being there. But I'd been counting down the days to this trip for months now. Missing that would be even worse.

Josh looked like he was actually in pain. "Dude, that's a whole year away!"

"Sorry," I said, getting up quickly. Dylan was already heading for the box of balls at the far end of the basketball court.

"Coach is not going to be happy!" Josh called after me, but I was already sorting through the bin, testing each ball with a bounce. Times like this, I wished I could just tell him the truth. But that would lead to a whole lot of other questions. Just thinking about them made my stomach hurt.

Using both hands, I slammed a ball down on the pavement hard, almost catching it in the face when it shot back up. Dribbling it, I asked, "So are we playing, or what?"

TWO

"Hey, I'm home!" I said loudly, closing the door behind me.

"Hi, honey!" Mom called back. "I'm with a client, be with you in a minute!"

I dropped my backpack on the hall floor and went to the kitchen for a snack. I was constantly hungry these days; watching me wolf down food, Mom always ruffled my hair and said I must be having another growth spurt. I really hoped she was right. I wasn't the shortest kid in my class, but I wasn't exactly tall, either.

I opened the fridge and scanned inside. Today the options were limited to soy yogurt, pickles, and hummus. Loading up my arms, I took them all over to the table.

Mom came in a few minutes later. When she saw

what I was eating, she laughed. "Seriously? Yogurt and pickles?"

"You work with pregnant ladies," I said defensively. "So this shouldn't seem weird."

Mom bent down and kissed the top of my head. "Not weird at all. In fact, maybe I'll join you."

Mom's a midwife who helps women have babies in their houses. Apparently I was born in a kiddie pool filled with warm water. I made Mom swear a blood oath to never tell my friends; if Josh ever found out, I seriously wouldn't hear the end of it.

Mom got a soy yogurt out of the fridge and pulled up a chair. Digging a spoon in, she eyed my head. "It might be time for another haircut."

I ran a hand through my hair self-consciously; ever since I turned eight, I've kept it super short, almost a buzz cut. She was right; it was much longer than usual. "Before we see Dad?"

Mom's eyes softened. "That's up to you."

I focused on my yogurt. "Let's go tomorrow after school."

"Great." Mom set the spoon on top of her napkin. "You know, you could always stay with me at Stella's."

"Dad's expecting me," I said without looking up.

"I know, but . . ." Mom tucked a finger under my chin, lifting it so I was forced to meet her eyes. "He's not always supportive, and I don't want you to feel like you *have* to stay with him. Okay?"

I nodded. To be honest, I was a little nervous about spending the weekend with Dad. I'd stayed with him for a full week over Christmas, and let's just say it hadn't gone very well. I'd only seen him once since then.

"Whatever you decide is fine," Mom said gently. "I can clear it with your dad."

"It's cool. I want to see him." I polished off my yogurt. "It'll be fun. He said he's got a surprise for me."

After dinner, I sat down at my desk and started drawing. I always lost track of time when I worked on my graphic novel; it was kind of like stepping into another, more exciting world. Not that my normal life was bad, but I wasn't exactly fighting aliens.

I'd started working on it last year. Before then I'd mainly messed around, trying to copy panels out of comic books. Major Victory, from the original *Guardians of the Galaxy*. Nova. Thanos. My favorites were sci-fi stories where the characters visited different planets, met strange new beings, and saw incredible things.

So the idea for my own graphic novel came from there. It was part *Guardians of the Galaxy*, part *Star Trek*, part *Firefly* (the best TV show ever, hands down). My hero was Hogan Fillion; Hogan, because that was the name of our dog when I was little, and Fillion after the actor who played Malcolm Reynolds, captain of the *Serenity* on *Firefly*.

Anyway, something terrible happened on Earth, killing pretty much everyone and making it uninhabitable. Hogan escaped in a spaceship and set off to find a way to save the planet. Along the way, he picked up an alien orphan that he named Willoughby. Willoughby is kind of like a hairless Ewok; but he shoots sparks when he's angry, which gets them out of a lot of tough situations.

Hogan doesn't have any special powers, but he's smart and funny and strong. He loves baseball (of course), and he loves Earth and he'll do anything to fix it. Along the way, they run into all sorts of aliens—some friendly, some not—and have a lot of adventures.

I'm almost done with it, which is kind of crazy. I thought it would take years, but I work on it every day after finishing my homework (and sometimes in class, which Mom wouldn't be happy about if she knew). On vacations and weekends, I draw for hours.

I know Josh doesn't totally get it. I've shown him a few pages, and all he said was, "Man, I wish I had muscles like Hogan."

Me too. In fact, I might've made Hogan too muscular, to make up for how scrawny I am.

Tonight I was finishing the final chapter. Hogan

has almost reached a planet where he hopes to convince the wise alien overlords to lend him technology that will save Earth. I was carefully penciling in Willoughby when Mom knocked on my door.

"Bedtime," she said.

"Sure," I answered. "Just one more sec."

She came in and peered over my shoulder at the outline of Hogan's ship, the *Maverick*, approaching a giant moon. "Wow, Shane. That's really good." Flipping back a page, she asked, "Who's this?"

"Uh, no one," I said, quickly turning the page back. She'd pointed to a panel where Hogan is kissing an alien girl with long red hair and purple skin. I'd realized after drawing her that she looked a lot like Madeline. Except for the purple skin, of course.

"I see," she said lightly. "Well, I can't wait to read it. What are you going to do with it?"

"Not sure," I said, carefully brushing eraser dust off my desk into my hand. "I haven't really thought about it." Actually, I had fantasies of sending it to Marvel. They'd be impressed enough to print a million copies, and then we'd be rich and famous. But realistically, I knew they probably wouldn't hire a twelve-year-old.

"Well, I think it's amazing." Mom kissed the top of my head. "Now go brush your teeth."

"Yes, sir," I said, giving her a mock salute.

After she left, I took a minute to look over the panels. I still had to figure out the ending, but I was close. Maybe when it was done, I could make copies and give one to Madeline. I wondered if she'd recognize herself.

THREE

"If we lose, I'm totally blaming you," Josh said as we walked out of class on Friday.

"Relax. You're playing the Cougars. You'll win."

"They beat us last year."

"Yeah, but last year you didn't have Austin." Austin was our best hitter, even though he was the smallest kid on the team. "He'll get, like, five home runs."

Josh frowned. "It'd still be better if you were playing."

"Course it would, 'cause I'm awesome," I said.

"Idiot," he snorted.

"Loser."

"It wouldn't hurt to address each other with respect, gentlemen," Señor Cordero said disapprovingly as we walked past him.

"*Sí, señor,*" Josh replied gravely. Turning back to

me, he said, "I respect you, Mr. Woods."

"I respect you, too, Mr. Choi."

Señor Cordero rolled his eyes, and we cracked up.

Josh nudged me as we approached the main gate. "You got time to play Call of Duty?"

I shook my head. "We're going straight to the airport."

"All right, then. See you."

"See you. And hey—don't lose."

Josh jabbed his fist at the sky, the code we'd come up with a long time ago that meant everything from *you're a jerk* to *catch you later*. "Team Shosh!"

"Team Shosh!" I answered.

There was a tug on my sleeve, and I turned to find Madeline smiling up at me. "Bye, Shane. Have fun in San Francisco!"

"Um, yeah, sure. Bye."

I watched as she crossed the street, bobbing slightly in her high-tops. A car honked; Mom was pulling our Volvo up to the curb. I hurried over and climbed in.

"How was school?" she asked, sounding distracted.

"Fine."

"Yeah?" Checking her mirrors, she carefully eased into traffic. "Is that all I get?"

I shrugged. "Pretty much."

Mom glanced over and gave me a small grin. "Remember when you used to tell me all about your day? I swear, you'd already be talking when you got in the car, and you wouldn't stop until you told me every single thing that happened. Including bathroom breaks."

"That was a long time ago, Mom," I said, embarrassed.

She reached out and squeezed my knee. "Well, I hate that you're growing up so fast."

"I wish it was faster," I grumbled. Maria was herding a bunch of kids across the street in front of us; Nico was with them, easily a head taller than everyone else.

Maria waved us forward, and Mom's forehead creased as she glanced at the clock. "Only two hours to our flight. Hopefully there won't be any traffic."

I settled back into my seat and closed my eyes. I could've sworn there was still a trace of strawberry bubble gum in the air.

"What are you thinking about?"

"What?" I asked, opening my eyes.

"The way you're smiling." Mom eyed me. "You looked like you were thinking about something nice."

I pointed to the GPS on the dashboard. "You better stay off the highway, it's already blocked up."

FOUR

"Coming!" Dad's voice boomed from behind the door. "Just hang on!"

Whenever we showed up, Dad always acted all stressed and surprised. As if he hadn't been expecting us, even though Mom had sent him two texts on our way from the airport.

"Would it have been too much trouble for him to pick us up?" she grumbled.

I threw her a look. "It was rush hour, Mom."

"You're right. Sorry." She tried to smile at me, but the corners of her mouth were tight, the way they always got around Dad. They weren't as bad as some of my friends' divorced parents; they never yelled at each other, at least not around me. But they always acted like strangers trapped in an elevator, awkward and eager to get out of there.

The door flew open and Dad filled the door frame. He was big, nearly six-four, with dark hair, broad shoulders, and a barrel chest. His arms were twice the size of mine; I always wondered if that happened overnight. Maybe one day I'd wake up and my hands would be able to grip a basketball as if it were an apple. He gave Mom a curt nod. "Rebecca."

"Adam," she said equally stiffly.

I fidgeted with the handle of my suitcase. Dad turned his focus on me. He always tried to hide it, but there was unmistakable disappointment in his eyes as he took me in. "Hey, kiddo. Wow, that's quite a haircut. You join the army without telling me?"

I could feel Mom bristling, so I eased past her and wrapped my arms around him. "Hi, Dad."

"Hi." He kissed the top of my head and gave me a big squeeze, so hard it felt like my ribs were getting crushed. "I missed you."

"Missed you, too, Dad."

Mom cleared her throat. "So his appointment is at noon tomorrow. I'll pick him up at eleven thirty."

"I can take him," Dad said, looking over my head at her.

Mom made a noise. "We've been through this. If he misses the appointment, they can't get us in for months."

"I said I'll get us there on time." Dad's voice had an

edge to it. "I don't know why you always act like—"

"It's fine, Mom," I interrupted, throwing her a pleading look. "I'll remind him."

Mom looked like she wanted to argue, but seeing my face, she just sighed. "All right. Don't stay up too late, okay?"

"Sure. Bye, Mom." I gave her a quick hug and stepped back. I'd learned a long time ago that the faster I could get them through this part, the better.

"Bye, Rebecca," Dad said without looking at her.

As he closed the door, Mom called out, "If you need anything, call me!"

"Yup!" I shouted back.

Dad shut the door, then looked at me appraisingly. "You're bigger."

"I guess." I wanted to tell him that I'd grown two inches since Christmas, but that seemed like something a little kid would say.

"So." He clapped his hands together. "Pizza for dinner?"

"Sure."

"Not that soy cheese nonsense your mom gets, either," he said, leading the way into the apartment. "I'll order from Goat Hill."

I wanted to defend Mom, but he was right; vegan pizza was kind of gross. "Great."

"All right, then." Dad's voice sounded a little fake,

like he didn't know how to talk to me. The first night was always awkward. Tomorrow would be better.

I left my bag in the hall while he went to order the pizza. Dad lived in a really nice apartment on the top floor of the building. I noticed it was tidier than usual, which was kind of weird.

I wandered into the next room, then stopped dead.

"Hey!" I said. "You got rid of the gym?" The treadmill, punching bag, and free weights were all gone. In their place was a long dining room table with matching chairs. He'd even hung art on the walls.

"Yup." Dad came and stood next to me, still holding the phone. "Thought it was time to have a real place to eat. You like it?"

"Sure," I said, although it had been kind of cool to have a gym in the apartment. Josh was super jealous when I told him about it. A dining room was boring in comparison.

"I got some new video games, too. Check them out. Hello?" He held the phone back to his ear. "Sorry about that. Half vegetarian, half pepperoni and sausage. Extra meat on that side." He threw me a wink.

I sorted through the stack of Xbox games in front of the TV while I puzzled over the order; Dad hated vegetarian pizza. Maybe he was on a health kick. I pulled out a box with a cloaked warrior on the cover and exclaimed, "The new Assassin's Creed? No way!"

"I thought you'd like that," he said, sounding pleased.

"I thought it wasn't coming out for another month!"

"A buddy snuck me an early copy." Dad grinned. "Want to play?"

"Oh, yeah. Definitely."

"I should have sent you one, too," he said guiltily. "You can take it, if you want."

"That's okay. I don't have an Xbox," I explained.

"Do you want one? I know you already had your birthday, but—"

I shook my head vigorously; I did all of my gaming at Josh's house. I could just imagine Mom's reaction to something as violent as Assassin's Creed. "I'm good. Let's play."

By the time the pizza arrived, we were almost back to normal. Dad had two specialized gaming chairs that were totally awesome, with speakers that blasted the sound right into your ears. I could tell he'd already been playing a lot, because he knew all sorts of tricks. He was definitely letting me win, but I didn't mind. I figured it made him feel better about not buying me an Xbox.

The doorbell rang again right after the pizza guy left, while I was getting plates and napkins. Dad suddenly looked nervous; he nearly spilled the milk he was pouring.

"Maybe he forgot something?" I suggested. "Did you remember to tip him?"

"Um, actually . . . I have a friend coming over." Taking in my expression, he said hurriedly, "I know, I'm sorry. I should've told you. But I think you'll really like her."

Her, I thought with irritation as he practically ran down the hall toward the front door. Dad had introduced me to a couple of girls over the past few years, but I never saw any of them more than once. I sighed.

Don't get me wrong, I actually don't mind that my parents date. They divorced when I was really young, so I don't even remember them together. And when they're with other people, my parents always seem happier. I actually really hope they'll both get married again someday.

But after not seeing Dad for months, I'd expected to have him all to myself this weekend. So I was in a pretty bad mood as I shuffled down the hall to meet his "friend."

I could hear her laughing at something Dad had said, as if he was the most hilarious guy in the world. When I turned the corner, she came into view: tall and blond like Mom, but much younger. She was way too dressed up for pizza night, too, in a skirt and heels.

"Shane, this is Summer," Dad said. I could tell

by his voice that he was worried about me saying the wrong thing.

I shook her hand. "Nice to meet you." It was limp in mine, like she didn't know how to shake properly.

"Hi!" Summer exclaimed. "It is *so* nice to meet you, too, Shane! I just love that picture of you in your dad's room!"

I threw him an accusing look: he'd promised to take that down the last time I was here. "It's my favorite," he said apologetically. "Besides, no one can see it in there."

No one but her, I thought, but didn't say it out loud.

"Is that pizza I smell?" Summer said, wrinkling up her nose like she was acting in a play. "I love pizza! And hey, I brought ice cream!"

I'd pretty much lost my appetite, so I picked at the pizza while they talked over me at the dinner table. Every time they asked me a question, I answered either yes or no. I could tell that Dad was getting annoyed, but I didn't really care.

It only got worse during dessert. Summer was scooping ice cream into bowls at the table. I was watching her hands, mainly so I wouldn't have to look at her face anymore. And that's when I noticed it. "Wow. That's a big ring."

Summer's eyes went to the giant diamond on her hand, then flicked over to my dad. They stared at each other for a minute, having one of those silent grown-up conversations. Then he leaned across the table and said, "Shane, there's something I need to tell you."

I already knew. Like I said, I don't have a problem with my parents dating, or even getting married to other people. It just hadn't felt very real until now.

"You're engaged," I said dully.

Another beat, then Dad took Summer's hand and said, "Yes, we are."

"And we want you to be in the wedding!" Summer said, trying way too hard to sound enthusiastic. "It's going to be next June."

"June?" I said, thinking, *I don't even know her last name.*

"We're thinking Napa," Summer continued. "Not too big, but I definitely have room for one more bridesmaid!"

And there it was.

It felt like I'd been punched in the stomach; suddenly it was hard to breathe. I stared at Dad, who was swallowing hard like something was caught in his throat.

"Oh," Summer said, putting a hand to her mouth. "I'm sorry, I just meant . . . of course, you don't even have to wear a dress if you don't want to. . . ."

I pushed my chair back so hard it fell over, then ran to my room. Slammed the door and fell back against it, breathing hard. Tears were stinging my eyes, and my nose was running.

A knock at the door. Dad said, "Shane? Listen, honey. Summer didn't mean anything by it, she just didn't understand some of our . . . rules. I told her you were a tomboy."

"I'm not a tomboy, I'm a boy!" I screamed, so loud it felt like the walls should shake and windows should shatter. My bedroom door didn't lock, so I stumbled into the bathroom and bolted the door. For a minute I just stood there, panting hard. My whole body was trembling. It was the worst thing my dad had ever done to me. I'd never felt so betrayed.

I sank to the floor, put my head on my arms, and cried.

WHA-

OOF!

WILLOUGHBY!

THE OVERLORDS!

THEY'RE INVISIBLE!

FIVE

When I was three years old, me and my friend Matt got into the glitter glue and basically covered ourselves with it, so my mom threw us into the tub to wash off. While she was getting towels, I noticed something. Pointing between Matt's legs, I asked, "What's that?"

"That's my peanut," he said proudly. "It's where the pee comes out."

This was pretty confusing for me, because it didn't look like a peanut; I was allergic, so my parents made sure I knew. "Can you eat it?"

Matt shook his head firmly. "It's a different kind of peanut, just for boys."

"But I don't have one, and I'm a boy," I pointed out.

"No you're not." He laughed. "You're a girl. That's why you have a pagina."

I frowned at him. "I'm not a girl."

"Are too."

"Am not!"

Matt splashed me, and I splashed him back, and he got soap in his eyes and started crying, so our moms came to get us. Which was probably for the best, because sometimes when Matt got mad he'd bite me, and I really hated that.

Later, when Mom was tucking me in for a nap, I'd asked, "Mommy, why don't I have a peanut like Matt?"

She bent over and kissed me on the forehead. "Because that's a boy thing."

"But I'm a boy."

She looked at me seriously. "Do you think it's better to be a boy?"

"No," I said, suddenly confused.

"It's okay to be a girl, too. You can still do any job you want, and marry whoever you want."

"I know. But I'm a boy."

"Okay. I love you, sweetheart," she said, giving me a hug.

That's when I discovered there's a difference between boys and girls, and that people thought I was the wrong thing.

After that, my parents were fine with me not

wearing skirts and dresses, and actually seemed kind of proud of the fact that I preferred to play with trucks and trains.

"She's a tomboy," they'd explain if anyone asked.

But apparently my dad was still telling people that; important people, like the girl he was going to marry. And that was definitely *not* okay.

After fifteen minutes, I got up and washed the tears off my face, avoiding the mirror. I used to cover it with soap, but he complained about the mess, so now I just kept my eyes down. I knew what I'd see there; at Dad's house, I always looked more like a girl.

I went back into my room and flopped down on the bed, chucking aside all the stupid stuffed animals that Dad insisted on buying me, like that would change anything. I could hear voices through the door and wondered if Summer was going to spend the night. I really didn't want to sit across from her at breakfast pretending everything was okay.

So I picked up the phone and called Mom.

Dad wasn't happy when Mom showed up a half hour later. They got into one of their whisper fights in the front hall, while Summer basically hid out in Dad's bedroom. I wondered if Mom even knew she was here; she definitely didn't know Dad was getting married, or she would've told me. I wondered if he was explaining that to her, too.

I held my suitcase handle as I waited in the living room, trying not to overhear even though it was hard because they were getting louder. Summer appeared in the door to my dad's bedroom. She looked like she'd been crying, too.

She forced a smile and waved for me to join her. I walked over as slowly as possible, hoping one of my parents would show up to rescue me before I got there.

"Hey," Summer said. Maybe she wasn't as young as I'd thought; she looked a lot older now, at least. "I kind of screwed up, huh?"

I shrugged, not trusting my voice.

"I just wanted to say I'm really, really sorry. Your dad—" She looked down the hall in his direction, even though he was still out of sight. "Well, he didn't explain everything to me."

"He didn't tell you his kid's a freak?" The words came out before I could stop them. I felt tears coming again and bit my lip hard to hold them back.

"Oh, Shane, you're not a freak." Summer bent low, like she wanted to hug me but wasn't sure if it would be okay. "You know, I have a niece who was born a boy."

I squinted at her suspiciously; that seemed way too convenient. "No, you don't."

"Well, more like a second cousin," she amended. "But we're really close. I never would've said that if I'd known."

I stared at the floor. It didn't really matter what she thought. She and Dad would get married, and they'd probably have a couple of kids—normal kids—and I'd end up seeing even less of him. "I hate my dad," I said in a low voice.

Summer looked startled. "Shane, you shouldn't—"

"I do, I hate him. And you can tell him I said that." I spun around and stormed down the hall. My parents stopped talking when they saw me. I pushed past Dad, ducking to avoid the hand he reached toward me.

"Shane, wait—" he said.

"I want to go. Now," I told Mom without turning around.

There was a long beat, then Mom said in a low voice, "I think it's best if I take him with me. We can try to straighten this out tomorrow."

Dad waited a long time before saying, "Okay." I couldn't tell if he was sad or relieved. Probably a little of both.

Mom didn't say anything until we reached the car. "Are you okay?" she asked as we got in.

I nodded. "I'm fine."

"You know you can talk to me about anything, right?" Which was what she always said when I didn't feel like talking. The thing she doesn't get is that talking doesn't always help; sometimes it makes things worse.

"I know, Mom. Now can we just go?"

She paused, then nodded and started the car.

SIX

I yawned and scuffed my sneakers against the chair legs while we waited. I'd been seeing Dr. Anne for four years now. She was a different kind of doctor; instead of colds and earaches, she worked with kids like me. Her office was really nice, with brightly colored walls, photos of kids, and interesting art all around. But even being here couldn't cheer me up after last night.

Mom was flipping through *Us* magazine and snorting to herself. Occasionally she'd raise her eyebrows and tilt a page toward me: *Celebrities: they're just like us!* or *Kim's new heartbreak*. She hated trashy magazines but always read them anyway while we waited.

There was a little kid sitting across from me, probably only eight years old. Her hair was still boy-short, but she was wearing a tutu and pink sneakers. Her mom sat stiffly with her hands folded on her lap, staring off at nothing, while the kid played a game on her phone. It made me feel funny watching them; I couldn't tell if the mom was happy to be here or not. Her lips were pursed tightly together, like she was waiting on bad news.

I took Mom's hand and gave it a squeeze. She threw me a surprised smile, then ran a hand over my hair. Leaning in, she said, "I love how it feels in the back after you've just gotten it cut, like a baby seal."

"Yeah, me too." I smiled back at her.

The door to the outer hall suddenly popped open, and we all looked up. No one was more shocked than me when Dad came in. Spotting us, he smiled uncertainly. "I wasn't sure if this was the right place. Man, what a maze!"

"Dad, what are you doing here?" I asked. After the way we'd left things, he was the last person I wanted to see.

"Doctor's appointment, right?" he said, looking pleased with himself.

Mom and I exchanged a quick look. He'd never come to a doctor's appointment before, not even when we still lived up here. He'd always had some excuse. I figured he must still be feeling guilty. I threw him a scowl. If he thought this would make up for last night, he was dead wrong. It was going to take a lot more than that.

Dad's tentative smile wavered when I didn't respond. He took the chair beside Mom and pulled out his phone. We sat there in an uncomfortable silence until Rainbow, my favorite nurse, walked around the reception desk. "Hey, Shane. Dr. Anne's ready for you."

I got up and slung my backpack over my shoulder, keeping my head low. My parents fell in step behind me. I saw Dad checking out the posters on the walls, which were mostly just pictures of kids. He seemed kind of relieved, which made me wonder what he'd been expecting.

"How's L.A.?" Rainbow asked, draping an arm across my shoulders as she led me back. I'd had a tiny crush on her ever since I was ten. She was beautiful, with light brown skin and blue eyes. She wore a little too much makeup, but even that couldn't cover how pretty she was.

"Cool," I muttered.

"I'll bet. You see anyone lately?"

I shrugged; she always asked the same question. "I saw some guy named Fabio in the grocery store. He was selling shampoo or something."

Mom and I thought it was pretty funny, this huge guy handing out tiny samples next to the kale. I hadn't known who he was. I'd actually thought he worked there; but Mom explained he was famous for being on the cover of cheesy romance books.

"Fabio, really?" Rainbow held out one of her long braids for me to examine. "You think his shampoo would work on my hair?"

"I don't know. He did have pretty nice hair," I offered.

Apparently that was a funny thing to say, because she laughed. "You're a real comedian, Shane." Rainbow tucked a file into the slot on the door as she held it open for us. "The doctor will be with you in a sec."

The door closed behind us. I sat on the examining table, and Mom took the chair. Dad plopped down on the doctor's stool, one of those rolling ones that spun. He turned in a slow circle. "She seems nice."

"Rainbow is awesome," I said.

"Great. And she's . . ."

Dad didn't say anything else, just sat there looking at us with raised eyebrows.

Before Mom could open her mouth to lecture him, I said, "Most of the people who work here are trans."

"Including the doctor?" Mom threw him a look, and he held up his hands defensively. "I'm just asking."

"Does it matter?" Mom said impatiently.

"I don't think she is," I muttered, equally annoyed. He was acting like this was a trip to the zoo or something.

"Well, I'm glad I'll finally get to meet her," Dad

said, in a big fake voice that was too loud for the small room.

I could tell Mom was steaming by the way she sat; shoulders tense, knuckles white on her purse straps. I was angry, too, but also felt a little sick. I really wished my dad hadn't come; it was ruining the whole thing. Thankfully, there was a sharp rap on the door, and Dr. Anne came in.

"Well, hello," she said. "All of you today, I see?"

Dad bounced off the chair as soon as the door opened, like he was afraid of getting in trouble for sitting on it. "Adam Woods. Good to finally meet you."

Dr. Anne shook his hand, then turned to us. "Hi, Rebecca, Shane. So great to see you again!"

"Hey," I mumbled, even though I wanted to say it was really great to see her, too. I had a regular doctor in Los Angeles for checkups, but Dr. Anne was my favorite. I'll never forget my first appointment. Mom had made me ask all these embarrassing questions, saying that Dr. Anne would have the answers, and wouldn't it be great to find out?

The big one was whether or not I'd ever be a "real boy."

I'd asked that question last, totally mortified the minute the words left my lips. I mean, I sounded like

Pinocchio or something. I waited for her to laugh me out of the room.

But instead, Dr. Anne sat down and looked in my eyes and said, "The most important thing to realize, Shane, is that you already are. You've got a boy's brain, and there are ways we can help you get the rest of it eventually, if you want. But all that stuff is the least important part about being a man. Does that make sense?"

I could tell she really understood. And it kind of made me think of things differently, too. Mom was always insisting that I hadn't been born in the *wrong* body, just a different one; a special one. That always seemed like total nonsense to me, but for some reason when Dr. Anne said it, it sounded right.

Now, she was lifting pages in my chart and nodding slightly, as if confirming something she already knew. "So you turned twelve a few months ago. Happy belated birthday!"

"Thanks."

"All right." Briskly, she closed the folder, adjusted her glasses, and looked at my parents. "Why don't you two step out for a minute while I do a quick exam?"

Dad looked disgruntled, but Mom was already gathering up her purse. After they left, Dr. Anne did the normal routine: checking my eyes and ears, pressing her fingers along my stomach and back. The whole time, she asked questions. "Still no side effects from the blocker?"

"Not really," I said. When I was nine, I'd started getting implants of a hormone blocker in my arm. "Just a headache every once in a while."

She nodded and flipped open the chart again. "And we put in the last one a year ago, so we'll switch that out for you today. So how have you been feeling lately?"

"Fine."

"No bad thoughts?" she asked, flipping over my arms to examine them.

"No, I'm good," I assured her. "Really."

She always snuck in these types of questions, because a lot of kids like me have issues. Mom and I used to go to a support group in L.A., until our weekends got too busy with baseball. One of the kids there was a cutter; another was so anorexic she looked like her legs could barely support her. "Body dysphoria," they called it; and it's why I used to see a therapist in addition to a regular doctor. I don't hate my body, though; I mean, I wish it was different, but it could be worse. There was a kid in my old school who was born with cerebral palsy; every move he made was jerky and wrong, and he couldn't play sports or anything. That would really suck.

"Great." Dr. Anne gave me a real smile then, showing all her teeth. "I think maybe it's time to decide whether to start the testosterone."

"Okay," I said, experiencing a thrill of excitement. This was the main reason we were here. It was why I'd been willing to miss such an important baseball game.

She patted my leg. "All right. Let's call your parents back in."

I kind of tuned out while Dr. Anne ran through the medical stuff. Dad nodded along, while Mom just looked bored and a little annoyed; we'd talked about all this before.

But then Dr. Anne got to the part about starting testosterone shots. "Most of the other boys Shane's age will be kicking into puberty high gear over the next year," she explained. "Ideally, it would be great if he could develop along with them."

"Sure, sure," Dad said, but I wondered if any of this was registering. Dad had a bad habit of acting like he was listening when he really wasn't.

"There are drawbacks, of course." Dr. Anne's eyes slid across to my mother, who suddenly looked worried.

Dad's forehead wrinkled. "What kind of drawbacks?"

Dr. Anne gave him a patient smile. "Basically, so far the hormone blockers have prevented Shane from going through female puberty. But once we add testosterone to the mix, he'll develop as a man. His voice will deepen, he'll get an Adam's apple and more body and facial hair, he'll be more muscular."

That all sounded great to me. I could hardly wait to start shaving; heck, I might even grow a mustache.

"Okay," Dad said slowly. "But if he stops taking the shots, that's reversible too, right?"

"Not entirely," Dr. Anne said. I could tell she was choosing her words carefully. "Some of the changes will be permanent. Others could be reversed surgically, or they'll just go away. But Shane will have skipped female puberty, which means he most likely won't be able to have children naturally."

There was a long moment of silence. I could see Dad processing this, and I didn't like the look on his face. "It's cool," I interjected. "Mom and me have already talked about it—"

"Wait," Dad said, holding up a hand. "You're telling me she'll never be able to have kids?"

"*He*," Mom growled. It drove her crazy when he used the wrong pronouns. Honestly, it drove me crazy, too, but in a different way. Kind of an all-the-air-sucked-out-of-the-room way.

"Not naturally, no," Dr. Anne said calmly. "And that's a serious decision."

"I'm fine with it," I said hurriedly. "Really, I—"

"You're twelve," Dad said. "You don't know what you want."

I stared at my sneakers, feeling sick. This all seemed to be spinning out of control, and there wasn't anything I could do to stop it.

"So we're supposed to decide this today?" Dad said incredulously. "It just seems really fast."

"We've been discussing it for a *long time* now," Mom said.

The way she said *long time* made it pretty clear what she meant, and she wasn't wrong. If Dad had ever come to a doctor's appointment before, this wouldn't be such a surprise.

Dr. Anne looked uncomfortable. "We don't have to decide anything today, of course. Shane can come back in six months, or a year."

"I think that would be best." Dad sat back, looking relieved.

"No!"

My parents looked at me with surprise, as if they'd forgotten I was in the room.

"Don't you get it? All the other boys in my class are going to be changing. The girls already have. And I'll still look like a little kid." Tears welled up in my eyes. "I don't want to be left behind."

"Shane, everyone develops at different rates. If we don't start today, it's not the end of the world," Dr. Anne said soothingly.

But it was. I'd been looking forward to this

appointment for months. After brushing my teeth at night, I'd stand in front of the mirror and puff my chest out, imagining how it would look once I started testosterone. I'd flex my puny biceps and picture them doubling in size. I'd practice deepening my voice until it almost sounded like Dad's.

And now, it was a wasted trip. Even worse, my team was probably losing without me, which meant our season would be over. And it was all my fault.

I stared down at the floor. One of the tiles was chipped. I focused hard on that, trying not to cry.

"Can we have a minute?" Mom asked in a strained voice.

"Of course." Glancing at her watch, Dr. Anne said, "Why don't I come back after checking on another patient?"

There was a heavy silence after the door closed behind her. Dad was looking everywhere but at us. Mom was glaring at him.

"I can't believe you," Mom finally said.

I stiffened. They had a rule about not fighting in front of me, but I got the sense that was about to be broken.

"This just caught me off guard." Dad ran a hand down his face. His eyes settled on me, and he tried to smile. "I guess I should've come to more appointments, huh?"

I shrugged. *Probably. Too late now.*

"This is the only reason we came up this weekend," Mom said, the anger plain in her voice.

"I don't see why waiting is such a big deal," Dad said defensively. "The doctor doesn't seem to think so."

"I do," I muttered.

"Shane, honey, I've been on board with all the rest of it. The blockers and . . . whatever." He waved his hand vaguely. "But this . . . I mean, it's so permanent."

Exactly, I thought. This would permanently make me who I was supposed to be all along.

"Well, we both have to agree," Mom said, "since we share legal custody."

Dad exhaled hard. He looked old, and tired, and in spite of everything I felt a pang of sympathy. He was trying, but this was all just too complicated for him sometimes.

Still, when he said, "I can't decide this today. Sorry," something withered inside me. Without looking at us he left, shutting the door behind him.

PLEASE...

YOU'RE THE LAST HOPE FOR MY PLANET.

WE DO NOT INTERFERE WITH THE DESTINY OF LESSER SPECIES.

AND YOU HAVE VIOLATED OUR LAWS BY COMING HERE.

BUT WE NEED YOUR HELP. I'LL DO ANYTHING!

WHIMPER

FOR THE CRIME OF INFILTRATING OUR BORDERS YOU SHALL BE SENTENCED TO SPEND THE REST OF YOUR DAYS...

... LOCKED IN SOLITUDE!

NO!!

SEVEN

All I wanted was to curl up in my own bed at home and cry; but our flight wasn't until the next afternoon, and Mom said it was too expensive to change the tickets. So we headed back to Stella's house.

Stella and Mom used to share a practice when we lived in San Francisco. Stella was tiny, with spiky blue hair even though she was seriously old, like fifty. She always wore ripped jeans and lots of spangly jewelry, and she did salsa dance in her spare time.

"Oh, Shane," she'd say, shaking her head. "You need to come take dance with me. If you know how to dance, when you get a little older? The girls won't be able to stay away."

I'd actually told Stella I was a boy first; it just kind of popped out one day when I was sitting in her kitchen, waiting for Mom. Stella was cutting veggies for a stew and going on about some guy she'd met in dance class. Then she'd asked, "What about you, Shane? You like any boys?"

I shook my head hard, suddenly aware of my cheeks flaming. Stella laughed loudly and said, "Aw, Shane, you can tell me! I won't tell your mother!"

"I don't like boys," I muttered.

Stella studied me for a minute, head cocked to the side; her bright blue hair made her look like a psychedelic rooster. "Girls, then?" she offered. Seeing the startled look on my face, she added, "No big deal for me, Shane."

"It's kind of complicated."

"Complicated how?" she asked, pulling up a chair.

I shrugged. But Stella wasn't the type of person who took a hint; she'd sit there all night waiting for an answer. So finally, in a low voice, I said, "Because I'm a boy."

It was strange, finally saying it out loud. I'd gone along with my parents calling me a tomboy forever, and this felt . . . different. Like when you drive too fast over a speed bump, and your stomach leaps up. I didn't dare look at Stella. I held my breath, waiting for her to say something, suddenly panicked that she'd tell my mom.

"Why didn't you say something sooner?" Stella cuffed my shoulder lightly. "Now I feel silly. All you had to say was, 'By the way, Stella, I'm a boy,' and then we'd have it all out in the open."

I was so overwhelmed with relief, I couldn't answer. I felt shaky and glad to be sitting down. "Don't tell Mom, okay?"

"It's up to you to tell her," she said. "But when you're ready, you should. Your momma, she's cool." She winked at me and stood back up. "Now finish your homework. I need help chopping."

And she was right, Mom had handled it pretty well—way better than Dad. Even now, years later, he still seemed to think this was some "phase" I was going through.

After we left the doctor's office, Mom offered to take me out for lunch, but I refused. I wasn't hungry. When we got back to Stella's house, I went straight to the guest room and closed the door. Mom had promised to try and convince Dad, but I didn't hold out much hope. I'd probably be on blockers until I was eighteen and legally old enough to decide for myself. Imagining six more years of this made me want to scream.

Afternoon sunlight flooded in, casting everything in a bright yellow glow. Stella's cat was asleep on a perch in the window. I rubbed his head while I stared out across the rooftops. A fog bank was descending from Twin Peaks, like an ominous cloud of white gas out of a horror movie, creeping across the city and smothering it block by block. Soon the house would be enveloped, and I'd barely be able to see across the street.

Which would match my mood, anyway. My phone buzzed and I dug it out of my pocket. There were two texts from Josh. The first read, Dude, we won!!! 4-2.

I should've been stoked about that—winning meant we'd go to regionals in a couple of weeks. But instead, I felt resentful that they'd been able to win without me. The next text said, Call me. It wuz totally awesome.

I tossed the phone on the dresser, not in the mood to talk to anyone. Instead, I lay down on the bed and glared at the ceiling. I'd never been so angry with my dad before. First, he surprised me with his new fiancée, then he completely destroyed something I'd been looking forward to for months.

I punched the pillow hard. If he didn't want a son, fine. Turned out I didn't really want a dad anymore, either.

EIGHT

At school on Monday, it looked like every-one had grown two inches. I knew it was just in my head, but even Josh's voice sounded deeper. The whole walk to school, he kept talking about how awesome the game had been. He'd hit a line drive to the gap in left-center, and they'd scored two runs off that, so Coach named him MVP.

"Wow," I kept saying. "That's really cool."

"What's wrong?" he finally asked.

I avoided his eyes. "Nothing, just . . . the trip kinda sucked."

"Sorry, man. You should've slept over."

"Yeah," I said, kicking a stone off the sidewalk. "I should've."

I was like a zombie in all my classes, because I'd barely slept the past couple of nights. At lunchtime,

I was getting stuff out of my locker when Madeline came over. "Hey! How was San Francisco?"

"Okay," I said. I could swear she looked older, too.

"Oh my God," she gushed, "the game was so awesome! Olive's brother scored a run."

"Yeah, we're going to regionals."

Her forehead creased. "Is something wrong?"

I shrugged. "I'm bummed I missed the game." The funny thing was, being depressed actually made it easier to talk to her, because I didn't care anymore about sounding like an idiot.

"I know. I wish I'd seen you pitch! Dylan was okay, but Olive kept saying you're better."

"Really?" Despite everything, I was flattered that they'd been talking about me. I wondered what else they'd said.

"Yeah." The bell rang and the hallway started emptying out. "Well, see you later!" She threw me a little wave before heading down the hall.

As I closed my locker, I turned to find Nico towering over me.

"Heard you made regionals. We did, too."

His breath smelled like eggs. "Cool," I muttered. I wasn't sure why Nico was even talking to me. I'd struck him out twice this season, so I wasn't exactly his favorite person.

"Now we just have to beat you losers for the

trophy." He smirked. "Coach says it'll be easy."

"Yeah, well, he's an idiot," I retorted.

Nico snorted. "He's a lot better than Coach Tom. I heard you skipped the game. Too scared to pitch?"

"No," I said defensively. "I had to go to San Francisco to see my dad."

"San Francisco sucks," Nico snorted. "My cousins live there and they hate it."

"So maybe they're losers."

"You'd know." Nico laughed at his own dumb joke. "Their school sucks worse than this place, too. It even has a stupid name: the Creative Academy."

"I went there, and it doesn't suck," I replied without thinking. Immediately, I realized I'd made a terrible mistake. I never told people about my old school, because everyone had known me as a girl there. My heart started hammering in my chest.

"Yeah? Do you know Josie and Cassie? They're in, like"—his brow furrowed as he did the math—"fifth and eighth grade?"

"Uh—nope," I said quickly, making a point of digging through my backpack. Actually, I did know them: two squinty-eyed mean girls. It figured they were related to Nico.

He frowned. "That's kind of weird. They said it's a small school."

"Not that small." It was getting hard to hide my

panic. Nico was giving me a funny look, like he sensed that I was lying.

"Whatever," he finally said. "And hey, you might want to miss regionals, too. Won't be a happy memory for you." He punched my shoulder hard enough to leave a mark before lurching away.

I zipped up my backpack and headed to class, my heart going a hundred miles a minute. When we'd first moved down here, I didn't think we could keep my secret for long (although Mom always insisted it wasn't "secret," it was "private"; apparently "secret" automatically sounded like a bad thing). I mean, we hadn't even changed my name, because I liked it so much, and it was kind of a boy name anyway.

But we got through fourth grade without anyone finding out, then fifth . . . and now, I hadn't even thought about it for a long time. I know that was probably dumb; after all, San Francisco wasn't very far away. But as more time passed, I became convinced that no one would ever know unless I decided to tell them. I'd even forget about being transgender for long stretches—that was the thing about finally being seen for myself: it made me believe in it, too.

And now, all it would take was Nico asking his cousins about Shane Woods, and I would be totally screwed.

———

It was a relief when the final bell rang and it was time to get ready for baseball. Even though we were a club team, we practiced on a field at school. Which worked out great for most of us, since more than half of the Cardinals went to McClane Junior High.

I changed in a locker room stall; thankfully, that had never been a big deal. A couple of the other boys were shy, so I was never the only one. I'd had a few close calls, but I'd learned to be careful. I always changed facing the back wall, and did it fast—I could strip off my pants, get my jock on, and have my baseball pants up in under ten seconds. Too bad they didn't give out prizes for that sort of thing.

When I slid open the curtain, Josh, Cole, and a couple of the other guys were still changing. They nodded at me and said hey. Grabbing my glove, helmet, and bat, I trotted out to the field.

As soon as the air hit me, it felt like my whole body got about fifty pounds lighter. There was something about that combination of freshly cut grass, dirt, and chalk that went straight inside me. Like a fish that gulps and gasps on a boat or dock, but throw it in the ocean and it's suddenly back in its element, moving and breathing the way it's supposed to. That's what a baseball field is for me.

The funny thing is, I hadn't even wanted to start

playing. Mom signed me up because she thought it would help me make friends.

The first day was a total disaster. I barely knew the rules and was painfully aware of being an outsider. Everyone else was talking about their favorite players and how their teams were doing, and I just sat there and listened, feeling like an idiot.

Josh was the only other new kid on the team, so the coach paired us up. He sent us to the outfield to throw a ball back and forth.

I was so clueless I hadn't even broken in my glove; the stiffness made it uncomfortable. Josh and I threw the ball, dropping more than we caught.

"You're the new kid, right?" he'd asked as I chased the ball to where it had rolled. The other boys were throwing their balls in long arcs that seemed to soar across the sky.

"Yeah."

"I hate baseball," he said morosely.

"Me too," I agreed.

"Cool. Hey, want to come over later to play Rise of Empires?"

This was the first time anyone had invited me over. Heart thumping in my chest, I played it cool. "Yeah, sure."

"Awesome."

Coach Tom ran us through some drills, trying to figure out what positions we'd play. In one of them, he had us try pitching. I watched the other boys carefully. The way they wound up looked weird, like they were about to topple over. Still, when it was my turn, I did my best to imitate it.

I threw the ball so hard it felt like my arm was going to come out of its socket. No one was more surprised than me when it smacked into the catcher's glove with a loud *slap!*

Coach Tom blinked, then said, "Hey, can you do that again?"

The catcher threw the ball back; I was so nervous, I nearly dropped it. But while the rest of the team watched, I threw it again, and again . . . each time it started to feel a little more natural. The coach finally nodded and said, "Nice work. All right, let's try hitting a few."

I wasn't nearly as good at hitting; that took longer to get the hang of. But Coach made me the team's pitcher, and suddenly, I belonged somewhere. Every night after I finished homework, I looked up stuff about baseball online. Pretty soon I was talking about the latest Giants game in the locker room. Before I knew it, I was totally hooked.

Josh turned out to be a great second baseman, and from then on we were best friends. We even came up with a goofy nickname, "Team Shosh," by combining our names.

That was three years ago, and now I can't even imagine life without baseball. Practice today was the only thing that might help me forget about Nico and his cousins.

Cole was our catcher; when I arrived on the mound, he was already waiting for me.

"Hey, man. You missed the game."

"Yeah, sorry."

Cole shrugged. "No worries. Hey, did you see that no-hitter last night?"

While we warmed up, we talked about the Giants game. The rest of the team was throwing balls back and forth: first base to second, third to outfield, outfield to shortstop. The Cardinals weren't the best team in our league, but we'd played together so long, it was like we could read each other's minds. Coach Tom always said that you didn't have to be the best, you just had to play your best.

Still, you could tell he was pretty pumped that we'd made it to regionals. None of his other teams had ever gotten this far. If we won, well . . . I couldn't even imagine how awesome that would be.

While I was winding up for the next pitch, I caught a flash of bright pink out of the corner of my eye. Distracted, I threw the ball wide.

"Ball!" Cole called out helpfully. I grimaced, then turned to see what it was.

Madeline and two of her friends were sitting on the top row of the bleachers. She waved at me enthusiastically. I flushed and nodded at her, then adjusted my cap. Suddenly I was totally self-conscious.

I tried not to let it distract me, but I was definitely off my game the rest of practice. Coach Tom called me over after I threw three balls in a row. He was about my dad's age, but shorter and with more of a belly. He squinted all the time, like the sun was constantly glaring in his eyes.

"All good, Shane?" he asked.

"Yes, sir. Sorry about that." I shuffled my feet. He'd made it clear on day one that no matter what we called other grown-ups, he was always "sir."

He worked the piece of gum in his mouth, then said, "You'll be ready for regionals, though, right?"

"Yes, sir."

"Good." He clapped me on the shoulder. "Why don't you take a few swings? I don't want to work that arm too hard."

I did better at hitting: two grounders, a fly, and one big hit to center field that was nearly a home run. I checked over my shoulder to see if Madeline was watching, but she and her friends were gone. I wondered if she'd been disappointed by my lousy pitching today; I knew I was. Somehow I had to get Nico and Dad and everything else out of my head, otherwise I might screw it up for the team at regionals.

As I walked back to the locker room, Josh trotted up and jostled me. "Man, you were a mess today."

"Gee, thanks." I pushed him back.

"Want to come over?"

I didn't answer, because my eyes had suddenly landed on a guy standing outside the locker room. I stopped dead.

Josh followed my gaze. "Hey, is that your dad?"

I was too shocked to speak. It had been over a year since he'd come to L.A. Dad waved at me.

"Didn't you just see him?" Josh asked.

His voice mirrored my worry, and I broke into a run. When I got to him, I asked breathlessly, "Is Mom okay? Did something happen?"

"What?" Dad's forehead wrinkled. "Oh, no, she's fine."

"Then why are you here?"

"What, I can't come see my kid?" He sounded hurt.

I was so thrown, it took a second to remember that I was still mad at him.

The rest of the team checked us out as they went by; few of them had ever seen my dad before.

Coach Tom came up. "This your dad, Shane?"

"Yes, sir," I mumbled.

Dad broke into a wide smile. "Hi, I'm Adam Woods."

"Your son's quite a player, you must be proud," Coach said, shaking hands. "Hope we'll be seeing you at regionals."

After he left, we stood there awkwardly. "So," Dad finally said. "There's a big game coming up?"

I nodded, annoyed. "Regionals, in a couple weeks. I told you about it."

"Oh." His eyebrows went up. "Well, that's huge, right?"

"Yeah." I scuffed the ground. *Why is he here? Did he change his mind?* I didn't want to get my hopes up, but a surprise visit was pretty weird.

Dad cleared his throat, then said, "Your mom said you can stay with me tonight if you want. I booked a room at the Marmont. It's supposed to be great."

After the way we'd left things in San Francisco, the thought of spending the night with Dad wasn't exactly appealing. I couldn't even look at him without feeling a swell of anger. I shrugged. "I don't have any clothes."

"We can swing by your mom's place to pack a bag," he said.

"Is Summer here, too?"

"Um, no." Dad looked abashed. "I thought it should just be the two of us."

That made me feel a little better, but not much.

"You know I've got school tomorrow, right? I have to be there at eight."

"I'll get you there on time, kiddo. Come on, it'll be fun." He reached a hand toward me. When I didn't take it, his face fell. "I'm parked over there. Let's go."

NINE

An hour later, we were sitting in a booth across from each other. We'd barely spoken during the drive over, and now that the waitress had left us alone, we were trapped in an awkward silence. Dad finally asked, "How's your burger?"

I pushed another fry through the ketchup on my plate. "Fine."

"Yeah? Your mom said this was your favorite place." Dad sipped his soda.

I didn't reply. The Counter has awesome burgers and shakes and sweet potato fries. But tonight, I was having a hard time choking any food down. I kept waiting for my dad to explain why he'd come, but so far he'd just asked about school and baseball. Like he was hoping that if we pretended nothing was wrong, everything would just go back to normal. *Not this time,* I thought, pushing my plate away and staring at the table.

Dad sighed. "So. You're still mad at me." When I didn't answer, he said, "Listen, Shane. I know it's hard for a kid to understand, but what you're signing up for with this hormone thing is a big deal."

"Could you not yell about it in here?" I snapped, scanning the full restaurant; it felt like everyone was listening. "And I know it's a big deal. It's pretty much all I've thought about for years."

He lowered his voice and leaned in. "Yeah, but . . . this is permanent. And it means giving up a lot, including some things that might not matter when you're twelve, but they'll be a pretty big deal later, trust me."

The anger boiled up inside me, but I kept my voice low. "So you want me to become a girl? Get breasts, and, and . . . a period?" I stared at him, dumbfounded. "No freaking way."

"But honey," he said, leaning across the table and staring intently into my eyes. "You *are* a girl. And maybe, if you just gave it a chance—"

I pushed back from the table and stood. "I want to go home."

"Shane, please," he said in a pained voice. "I really want to work this out."

"No, you don't," I retorted. "You just want me to be something I'm not."

I stormed out of the restaurant. I wanted to keep going, through the parking lot and down the street. But home was miles away, and Mom would be upset about me walking alone after dark. I could call her, but then I'd still be stuck waiting with Dad. So I stood by the rental car, glaring at the ground while he paid the bill.

When my dad finally came out and unlocked the doors, I slid in and fastened my seat belt without saying anything. He didn't start the car right away. Instead, he sat there, staring out the windshield.

"Take me home," I repeated forcefully.

"I will. Just . . . please, give me a minute." His fingers were white on the steering wheel. "Do you remember the fairy horse?"

"What?" I asked, confused.

"The fairy horse." He gave me a tentative smile. "You were probably three years old, and we'd gotten you this horse costume for Halloween. And you insisted on wearing it everywhere for months. We'd be in the grocery store, and someone would say, 'Oh, what a cute little horse,' and you'd yell, 'I'm a fairy horse!'"

I knew what he was talking about; Mom had shown me pictures. "What's your point?"

"You had all these stories, too. When you came to wake us up every morning, you'd spend ten minutes telling us about all the adventures fairy horse had the night before. You'd rescued kittens from trees, you'd fought dragons . . . it was pretty incredible, the stuff you came up with." He smiled. "Do you remember that?"

"No," I said, mentally willing him to just start the car already.

Dad sighed again. "I know it sounds selfish, but what I'm getting at is that for a long time, you were my little girl."

"But—"

"I know," he said, holding up a hand to cut me off. "You weren't a girly girl, we knew that right away. I think you liked the horse costume because you didn't want to wear skirts or dresses anymore. I never really cared about any of that. But in some ways, I guess it feels like I've lost my little girl. Sitting in that doctor's office, all I could think was that we were saying good-bye to her forever."

I examined my hands, feeling awful. Like I'd disappointed him by not being the kid he'd wanted; and angry that he was making me feel that way. No matter how many times I'd tried explaining it, I couldn't convince him that the little girl he remembered had never actually existed. "So you wish I was a girl, and now you're forcing me to become one."

"That's not it at all." He rubbed the bridge of his nose. "I'm messing this up, aren't I?"

"Yeah, basically," I muttered.

"Well, I'm trying, Shane."

I glared at him. "What if you woke up tomorrow, and someone had switched your body while you were asleep?"

"What, like a *Freaky Friday* thing?" He looked perplexed.

"Yeah, sure. And suddenly, you had a girl body. Would you automatically feel like a girl? I mean, you'd have the same brain. All that changed was your body."

He looked uncomfortable. "I don't know. I mean, I wasn't born that way—"

"But neither was I!" I said impatiently. "I was born with a boy brain, just in the wrong body. It sucks."

He sat there for a long time. Other people were coming out of the restaurant, chattering and laughing with each other. The silence in the car felt heavy and thick. Finally, he said, "I guess I never really thought about it that way."

"Well, that's how it is," I muttered. "So I'm not trying to be something I'm not. I've always been like this."

"Maybe if we just wait a little longer—"

"It won't make a difference," I said, exasperated. "I'll just do it on my own as soon as they let me. Now can we go already?"

He still didn't start the car. Again I debated getting out and walking, figuring I'd rather be in trouble with Mom than have to sit here for another five minutes.

"All right," he sighed.

"All right what?"

He gave me a weak smile. "If you really understand what this means, what you're giving up, well . . . it's your body. Your life. I just worry that you'll end up regretting it."

I practically stopped breathing. "You mean it?"

"Like you said, you'll eventually do it anyway. At least this way, maybe you won't end up hating me."

He looked sad, but I didn't care—I threw my arms around him. "I love you."

"I love you too, kiddo," he said thickly. "You're my whole world."

I'M SORRY, WILL. THIS IS ALL MY FAULT.

#5%¿.

HEY, THERE'S NO NEED FOR THAT KIND OF LANGUAGE.

WHAT NOW?

COME QUICKLY. I CAN HELP YOU, BUT THERE'S NOT MUCH TIME.

SEE, WILLOUGHBY? I TOLD YOU IT WOULD BE OKAY!

#¿5*%?!

SURE WE CAN TRUST HIM!

COME ON!

TEN

I was pretty bleary at school the next day, because Dad and I stayed up late eating junk food and watching a movie about alien robots. But I felt about a million times better. On the phone last night, Mom promised to talk to Dr. Anne about the testosterone. She said we might even be able to get it in a day or so.

I couldn't stop thinking about it. Dr. Anne had said the changes might take time: it would be just like regular puberty, and everyone went through it at different rates. But I was kind of hoping I'd at least start growing chest hair, like Dad.

Dad promised that the next time I visited, we'd go somewhere fun with Summer, maybe even to a Giants game. He kept talking about how nice she was, and how much she'd liked me, which was ridiculous, since we'd barely said two words to each other. I wanted to tell him not to try so hard, but we were both in such a great mood I decided not to risk ruining it.

I was feeling so good that when I saw Madeline at her locker after first period, I did something that qualified as either incredibly brave or incredibly stupid. I walked boldly up to her and said, "Hey."

"Hey!" She turned and smiled at me, nearly dropping the stack of books she was holding. I reached out and helped straighten them. "Thanks."

"I saw you at practice yesterday," I said, leaning against the locker next to hers.

"Yeah, I went with Olive." Madeline's eyes went wide. "Wow, you throw the ball really fast! Are you, like, really, really good?"

I flushed. "I guess I'm okay. Are you coming to the next game?"

"What, the regionals? Yeah, sure."

"Cool." I nodded a few times, trying not to let the excitement show on my face. "Hey, I was wondering if you wanted to go to a movie or something?"

"What?" She stared at me like I'd just said something completely crazy.

"Um . . ." My cheeks burned. "The new *Fast and Furious* is supposed to be pretty good."

"The one with the cars?" Her forehead wrinkled.

"Or whatever," I said quickly. How did people do this? On TV, when a guy asked a girl out, he was always really slick about it, and she always said yes. Madeline looked just as uncomfortable as I felt; I could tell she was trying to figure out what to say. "You know what? It's cool. Forget it."

I started walking away, but Madeline called after me, "Shane, wait!"

"Yeah?" I asked, turning around.

Coming over, she said in a low voice, "Um, it's totally lame, but my parents think I'm still too young to go out with a boy."

"Oh, okay." A rush of relief flooded over me.

"But maybe . . . I mean, if you want, you could come over and study sometime? I think they'd be okay with that."

"Yeah?" I was pretty sure she could hear my heart thudding around my chest like a crazed bat. "Cool."

"I'll ask today, okay?" She smiled at me.

"Sure."

"Great. See you later." She gave me a little wave and walked off. I stared after her, feeling like gravity had released me and I was floating a couple of inches above the ground.

"What's going on?" Josh asked, coming up behind me.

"Huh? Nothing." I adjusted my backpack straps.

"You look funny," he said suspiciously. "Like, all smiley."

"I am not." I forced a scowl.

"Whatever, dude. Gotta warn you, there's a pop quiz in Spanish."

That brought me down quick. "Seriously?"

"Yup. Dylan said Señor Cordero gave one in first period, so we'll have it, too."

"That sucks," I muttered. I hadn't studied at all last night. Dad and I had been too busy.

"Totally." Josh walked down the hall with me. "Want to come over after practice?"

"Um, I can't."

He stopped, a hurt look on his face. "Why not? I've got the new Anomaly."

"Sorry, I've got to hang out with my mom." The truth was, I couldn't wait to find out what Dr. Anne said. I wouldn't be able to pay attention to anything else.

"All right, weirdo," he said, rolling his eyes. "Tomorrow?"

I hesitated; what if Madeline got permission for me to come over then? "Maybe."

Josh stared at me, looking puzzled. "Are we cool?"

"Yeah." I pumped my fist up the way we usually did.

But he didn't do it back. Sounding annoyed, Josh said, "Whatever," and walked away.

"Hey, Josh, wait." But he didn't stop. I watched as

he pushed through the double doors to the stairwell without looking back.

Madeline showed up to watch practice again. She kept waving at me from the bleachers, which made her friends dissolve into giggles. I waved back once, then tried to avoid looking at her. It was hard, though. I played better than yesterday, but not by much.

Josh kept looking back and forth between me and Madeline, wearing a sour expression like something smelled bad. In the locker room after practice, he barely spoke to me. I wasn't sure why he was so upset; when I tried to talk to him about it, he brushed me off. *He can never stay mad for long,* I told myself. Still, it was hard because we almost never fought.

Mom picked me up after practice. I practically ran to the car, and before the door was shut I asked breathlessly, "So what'd she say?"

Mom laughed. "Well, hello to you, too."

"Hi, Mom. I love you. Now what did Dr. Anne say?"

Mom reached out and tugged the rim of my ball cap. "How was practice?"

I groaned. She was smiling, so it had to be good news. Typical Mom, she'd drag it out just to torture me. "It was fine. What did the doctor say?"

"Asking over and over won't make me tell you any

faster," she said breezily. I made an exasperated noise as she turned onto the main road.

"How's your dad?"

"Fine."

"And the Marmont?"

"Fine."

"Ah, so we're playing that game," she said knowingly. "What about math?"

I made a face; she knew I hated math. Gritting my teeth, I said, "Fine."

Mom laughed again. "By the way, who was that girl?"

"What girl?"

"The cute redhead who waved at you."

"Madeline," I muttered.

"I've always loved that name," Mom said. "So what's Madeline like?"

I scrunched down lower in my seat. "I don't know. Nice."

Her voice got serious. "Do you like her?"

"Like her?"

"You know what I mean. I don't know, are they still calling it a crush these days?"

I buried my face in my hand. "This. Is. So. Embarrassing."

"Aw, c'mon." Mom reached out and squeezed my

shoulder. "You're not a teenager yet. Tell me something, at least."

"I did. I told you she's nice."

"Okay." Quirking an eyebrow, she added, "Fine."

Then she took a left instead of a right.

"Um, Earth to Mom? We're going the wrong way."

"We are?" Mom feigned innocence, her eyes wide. "Are you sure?"

"Mom, seriously. I need to get home and do homework."

She took a left into a drugstore parking lot. "I thought you wouldn't mind if we made one quick stop."

I suddenly realized this was our usual pharmacy. "Wait—"

Mom broke into a wide grin. "Your prescription should be ready. Dr. Anne called it in at lunchtime."

I threw my arms around her. "Thank you, thank you, thank you so so much. . . ."

Mom hugged me back. Her eyes were a little misty when she finally pulled away. "I know, best mom ever, am I right? Now let's go get your medicine."

ELEVEN

"And just like that, you're dead," Josh crowed.

I growled and hit the reset button. "No fair. You already did this level."

"Hey, you could've come to play yesterday," Josh said with a shrug. We were sitting on his living room floor in front of the TV, watching the pinwheel spin as Anomaly reset. "How was hanging with your mom?"

"Fine," I said, repressing a twinge of guilt. Keeping this huge part of my life from him was really hard. I'd come close to telling him so many times but always chickened out. I was terrified that even if Josh pretended it was okay, he'd act different around me. That happened with some of my friends in San Francisco. I didn't think I could stand it again.

"Hey," he said, throwing a chip at me. "What's wrong with you?"

"Nothing," I muttered, tossing it back.

"You've been weird lately." The game restarted, and we both maneuvered our tanks toward a tower. "Is it because of Madeline?"

"What?" I said, startled.

"Please." He rolled his eyes. "Just admit it already— you like her. Hey, watch out, that's an ambush!"

I groaned as my convoy was blasted apart again. "Man, this is harder than the last version."

"Yeah, but better, too." He pressed a button to reinitiate the start sequence. "So?"

"So what?" I said.

"You like Madeline?"

I shrugged. "Yeah, I like her."

"Yeah, but do you *like her* like her?" he said in a high, fake voice.

I frowned and mumbled, "I don't know. I mean, she's cool."

"Yeah, she's all right." Josh was facing the game again, not looking at me.

"What?"

"Nothing." The hurt was plain in his voice. "I mean, it's pretty obvious you don't want to talk about it."

I struggled to think of what to say; this was easily

the most uncomfortable conversation we'd ever had. "It's not that I don't want to talk about it. It's just . . . weird, you know?"

His shoulders relaxed slightly. "Yeah." After a beat, he added, "You're weird."

I snorted. "No weirder than you."

"Oh, you're definitely weirder than me." He threw me a sidelong grin. "Hey, did your mom give you the talk yet?"

I rolled my eyes. "Dude, my mom's a midwife. I got the talk when I was in diapers."

Josh laughed, then said, "My dad came into my room the other night. I thought he was going to say something really bad, like they were getting divorced, because he looked so nervous. Then he asked if I had a crush on a girl."

"Seriously?"

"Yup. And when I said no, he asked if I had one on a guy."

I started to laugh, then caught myself. "Do you?"

He threw me a surprised look. "No."

"Because it's cool if you do."

Josh groaned. "Oh my God, that's exactly what Dad said. No, man, I like girls. I mean, I don't like one of them more than the others, but I'm not gay. I'd tell you if I was."

My heart was pounding. If I'd ever wanted to come

clean, this was pretty much the perfect time.

But what if he freaked out? The pressure built in my chest, and my stomach twisted. I tried to figure out what to say, and how to say it.

Onscreen, my tank blew up again.

"Dude! You suck!" Josh laughed and punched my shoulder.

The moment had passed. Relieved, I swallowed hard and said, "I do kind of want Madeline to be my girlfriend."

"I knew it!" he exclaimed, sitting up so fast he knocked over the bag of chips. "And she likes you too, right?"

"I don't know," I admitted. "I think I'm going to study at her house sometime."

"*That's* why you didn't want to come over," he said shrewdly. After a long beat, he asked, "So what does that mean?"

"Huh?"

"I mean, what do you do with a girlfriend? Hold her hand and stuff?" Josh looked embarrassed, like he should know the answer.

"I don't know. Maybe."

Josh leaned in and said, "I heard Brooklyn let Nico get to first base."

"Really?" There were lots of rumors about Brooklyn, which was probably why she always looked kind of sad. I hesitated, then asked, "What's first base again?"

Josh stared at me for a beat, then burst out laughing. "I don't know! I thought you did."

"Why, because I like Madeline?" I laughed too. "Hey, maybe you should ask your dad."

That set Josh rolling around on the floor. We were both laughing so hard, it was tough to breathe. Finally, through gasps, he said, "Some baseball experts we are. We don't even know what the bases mean!"

That set us off again. Josh's mom appeared in the doorway. "What's so funny?"

"Baseball!" Josh barked. We both collapsed in giggles.

She stared at the mess we'd made: pretty much the entire bag of chips was crushed into the carpet. "Josh! Clean this up!"

"Okay, Mom."

"Sorry, Mrs. Choi," I gasped.

We crawled around on our hands and knees, scooping the bigger pieces back into the bag. Every time we caught each other's eye, we'd start cracking up again.

While Josh went over the carpet with the vacuum, I checked my phone. "Oh, man. I've got to get home."

"Yeah, almost dinnertime," Josh agreed. "No chips tonight!"

We both snorted. Then he gave me a serious look. "You know, you could've just told me."

I pulled on my backpack. "I guess I felt weird about it."

"Well, don't." Josh stood up and clapped me on the shoulder. Imitating Señor Cordero, he said, "My leetle boy is becoming a man."

I slapped his hand away, and he cuffed me on the side of the head.

"See you tomorrow?" I said from the doorway.

"Yeah. See you."

The next morning I examined myself in the mirror, lifting my arms and flexing my biceps. Then I leaned in to check if I'd sprouted a mustache yet.

Nothing, which was a little disappointing. Mom had given me the first shot as soon as we got back from the drugstore. I'd never liked needles, but this one was pretty small and hadn't hurt much. And heck, I'd do pretty much anything for chest hair.

When Dr. Anne had explained over Skype how testosterone worked, she'd warned that it would take time to notice any changes. I'd jokingly asked if doubling up on the shots would make it go faster; she'd laughed, but then got really serious about how bad things could happen. "Just stick to the dosage, Shane," she'd said. "Trust me, it'll all come in time."

Easy for her to say—she wasn't in junior high.

At least *something* was happening, even if I couldn't

see it yet. I pulled on a shirt and took the stairs two at a time. Mom was in the kitchen, holding her head in both hands. When she saw me, she smiled weakly. "How are you feeling, honey?"

"Fine, Mom. Normal."

"Good."

"Rough night?" I asked. Mom had been called out on a birth right after dinner.

"First-timers," she said with a sigh, taking a sip of coffee. "No baby yet. I'm heading back there soon. I'll text you if I'm going to be late."

"Sure." I leaned over and kissed her. "Good luck."

She gave me a little wave.

Josh was already gone when I got to his house. That was cool; we had a deal where if I was more than five minutes late, he left without me. And today, I was way behind. I broke into a trot, then a full run when I heard the first bell from the crosswalk.

First period was kind of weird; I could've sworn people were staring at me, but every time I checked, they were all focused on the blackboard. I shrugged it off; Dr. Anne had said the shots might make me feel edgy.

After class, I spotted Madeline's red hair through the crowded hallway. Breaking into a grin, I pushed through the mob.

"Hey!" I said when I reached her.

Madeline smiled up at me. "Hey. I talked to my parents. They're okay with you coming over, but we have to study in the living room. And they want to meet you first."

"That's cool," I said, although the thought was terrifying. *What if they don't like me?*

"My mom wants to know if you can come over for dinner tomorrow night."

"Yeah, sure," I said. Tomorrow was Friday, which was usually pizza and movie night with Mom, but I figured she'd understand. "What time?"

"Like, six o'clock?"

"Sounds great," I said, trying to act casual.

"Okay."

We were smiling at each other. Should I lean in and try to kiss her cheek or something? Maybe squeeze her shoulder? Did this mean she was officially my girlfriend?

It was all so confusing.

I was distracted by a couple of people staring at us. When I caught their eye, they looked away and walked faster. *Edgy,* I reminded myself. They probably weren't really looking at us at all.

Madeline was frowning when I turned back to her. "What?"

"Oh, just . . . there's a stupid rumor going around." She looked uncomfortable.

I froze. "What kind of rumor?"

"Nothing. Just that idiot Nico," she said dismissively. "His cousins told him something crazy, and now he won't shut up about it. Ignore it and it'll go away. Anyway, I'm late for pre-algebra. Bye!"

I stared after her. The bell rang. People hurried past me, their chatter sounding abnormally loud. I waited until the hall had cleared entirely, then walked to the bathroom on wobbly legs.

It was empty, thank God. I went into a stall, closed and locked the door, and sat on the toilet seat with my head in my hands. It felt like I was going to be sick. Nico was spreading a rumor about me. His cousins went to my old school. Josh hadn't waited for me this morning. People were staring and whispering.

Ignore it, Madeline had said. *It'll go away.*

But deep down, I knew it wouldn't. I'd been waiting years for this to happen—dreading it—and now, at the worst possible time, my secret was out.

I was hit hard by a wave of vertigo. The bathroom stall seemed to lengthen as the walls pressed in, like the trash compactor scene in *Star Wars*. I couldn't breathe, my chest shuddered as I tried to suck in oxygen that wouldn't come.

Over and over, the roar in my head: *they know.*

TWELVE

When I was in music class in third grade, the teacher asked us to divide up into boys and girls. We were supposed to sing, "Free to Be . . . You and Me" for the next assembly, and there were different parts for each gender.

I don't know what made me do it, but heart pounding, I climbed up to the boys' riser. Ms. Cathy said, "Shane, you're in the wrong row."

"No, I'm not," I said in a squeaky voice.

A few of the kids laughed; they thought I was trying to be funny.

Ms. Cathy tilted her head sideways, looking surprised. "I'm not kidding, Shane."

"I'm not, either."

At that, the class got really silent and still. The other kids were staring, eager to see what would happen next. Ms. Cathy didn't seem to know what to do. She just kept frowning at me. After a minute, she cleared her throat and said, "All right, let's take it from the top. Shane, we can talk after class."

Ms. Cathy was one of my favorite teachers. She always wore wraparound skirts and scarves, and she smelled like spices. She was younger than the other teachers, too, which made her a lot nicer in general.

"So is anything wrong, Shane?" she asked once everyone else had filed out.

"No." I stared at the floor, already regretting it. I should've just kept my mouth shut and gone with the girls.

"Are you sure? Because this is really unlike you."

"I'm sorry," I said. My voice seemed to bounce off the walls, the high ceiling, the drums in the corner. Tears tugged at my eyes.

"You don't have to be sorry. I'm just trying to figure this out." Her brow wrinkled. "Were you trying to be funny?"

I slowly shook my head.

"Okay." She bit her lower lip. "Then why did you want to go with the boys?"

Up until that point, I still hadn't told anyone but Stella. This felt safe, though. Ms. Cathy seemed like the kind of person who would understand. So I drew in a big breath and said, "Because I'm really a boy."

"I see. And do your parents know?"

I slowly shook my head.

"Okay." Ms. Cathy sat there for a long time, rapping a tempo on the desk with her fingertips. Finally, she said, "You know what? Next class, I'm going to tell everyone they can take whatever part they want; splitting into boys and girls was kind of a silly idea anyway."

"Okay," I said, relieved.

"And Shane, I promise I won't say anything to anyone. But, well . . . I've met your mom, and she seems like a good person to talk to about this sort of thing. Don't you think?"

I nodded, even though the thought of telling Mom still terrified me.

When Mom picked me up from school that day, I was a mess. I couldn't stop worrying that, despite her promise, Ms. Cathy had called her. Plus, my classmates were acting weird around me. At recess, a few of them asked why I'd gone with the boys; I didn't know what to tell them, so I said I was just kidding around. But they didn't all believe me.

Anyway, I was quiet the whole way home, and Mom kept asking if something was wrong. When I refused my snack, she sat me down at the kitchen table, and it all came out. I told her about what happened in music class. I confessed that I hated looking in mirrors because my hair was too long and made me look like a girl. I explained that I didn't want to do ballet anymore, because only girls took that.

Mom just sat there and listened. I couldn't tell what she was thinking. Her face was kind of closed, which was the scariest part. But then she pulled me onto her lap and hugged me, and said, "I'm so glad you told me."

"You're not mad?" I asked, sniffling. Somewhere along the line I'd started crying, and I couldn't seem to stop.

"Of course I'm not mad, sweetheart. But I don't know much about this. So why don't we try to find out more?"

The next week she took me to see my first therapist, a nice lady named Diane who specialized in kids like me. She asked a lot of questions, like when I'd known I was a boy, and what the difference between boys and girls was. She had all these cool toys in her office, and she let me play with them. It was a huge relief to finally be open about everything; it felt like this enormous weight had been lifted.

After my first session, Mom took me to get my hair cut short. I swear I'd never been so happy. Other than that, not much changed. I still played with my friends, Mom and I still had movie night, Dad still brought me to the zoo. I hadn't told him yet; Mom said I could wait until I felt ready.

We ended up telling him together, in Diane's office. He took it pretty well; of course, looking back, now I know that he expected me to grow out of it. That first year he kept buying me girl clothes and toys, like that would make it go away.

Mom sat me down over Christmas break and said that it might be time to tell people at school. She called it "transitioning," which basically meant letting everyone know I was really a boy. I didn't want to at first, but she pointed out that I shouldn't have to keep pretending to be something I wasn't. "I'll make sure the teachers help everyone understand," she promised. "And if there are any problems, we'll handle them together. Okay?"

I was nervous—actually, more like petrified—but in the end, it wasn't as bad as I thought it would be.

The thing about third graders is that they're generally pretty easy; if you tell them you're a unicorn, they just go, "Oh, okay," and you keep playing. I was kind of surprised by how well everyone took it. They didn't always get the pronouns right, but they tried, and that mattered.

By the end of the year, it seemed like everyone was used to it. No one stopped being my friend or anything like that. I even accidentally got into a real fight; we were playing dodgeball, and this fourth grader threw the ball too hard, so I pushed him. He turned around and punched me in the chest, knocking me over.

Mom was pretty mad about that, and he ended up getting in a lot of trouble. But even though it hurt, I was really psyched that he'd treated me like a boy; he never would've hit a girl. And weirdly, that made me feel good, like I was finally being seen for who I was.

So when Mom announced that we were moving to L.A. because there would be more work for her there, I was devastated.

I barely spoke to her the whole summer. Watching all my stuff get packed up, having to say good-bye to the room I'd lived in since I was born—that was really, really hard. Mom kept trying to cheer me up, saying that I'd be in a great new school, with a public pool right down the street, but it didn't matter. I was convinced she was ruining my life.

That was when she said that if I didn't feel like it, I wouldn't have to tell anyone at my new school. She called it "stealth mode," like I was a bomber jet or something. Apparently a lot of other trans kids did that, and it usually worked out fine. Still, I didn't really trust that it would for me.

Looking back, I'm sorry I acted like such a brat. Because moving turned out to be the best thing we could've done. I walked into fourth grade wearing basketball shorts and sneakers, my Volcom backpack over my shoulder, and everyone just saw me as a boy. I wasn't the "special" boy anymore; everyone treated me like I was normal. Until then, I hadn't even realized how different it had been at my old school. Sure, they'd been great, but they still behaved like I was fragile and had to be handled carefully. I don't blame them for that; it's just how it was.

Now it was hard to remember my life in San Francisco; sometimes it felt like a dream.

I walked out of the bathroom and left school without telling anyone. I'd never done anything like that before. I thought about going to the nurse, but she'd call Mom, and I really just wanted to be alone.

I walked home slowly. There weren't many cars on the streets, and the only people I passed were moms with strollers. It was a beautiful day, warm and sunny, but all I could see was gray.

I opened the door with my key, dumped my pack on the floor, crossed to the couch, and collapsed on it.

I don't know how long I stayed there. I kind of lost all sense of time. I couldn't get up the energy to watch a show, or to eat anything. I just lay there staring at the ceiling, wondering what to do. The options seemed pretty limited, and none of them were great.

I could just lie and say that Nico was wrong, his

cousins didn't know what they were talking about, they were confused. The problem was if he made any sort of effort, it would be easy to prove. Anyone who went to the Creative Academy could find pictures of me with long hair. And if Nico brought those in and passed them around, it would make things even worse.

I could do what Madeline said and just ignore it. Unless people asked straight out, and not many probably would, it would just be a rumor. Kind of like last year, when everyone was talking about how Jordan Taylor's arm had been broken by his dad, not in a skateboarding accident like he'd said. Once the cast came off, though, people seemed to forget about it. That could work, for a while; but what if Josh asked, or Madeline? Would I have to lie to them, too?

Or we could move again, which seemed like the best option. We could even go back to San Francisco, but to a different school. I'd legally change my name this time, and would just avoid everyone from our old life.

Of course, then I'd be leaving the baseball team, and Josh. But there were club teams in San Francisco, I told myself. I'd started over before. I could do it again.

I must've fallen asleep, because the next thing I knew, Mom's cool hand was on my forehead. I opened my eyes; she was perched next to me on the couch, looking worried. There were deep circles under her eyes, and her hair was tied back in a messy bun.

"Did they have the baby?" I croaked.

She broke into a smile. "A little girl." Mom moved her hand down to my cheek. "Why are you home already? It's only two o'clock."

"I felt sick," I said.

Mom tilted her head. "I didn't get a call from the nurse."

"I didn't go to the nurse," I muttered. "I just came home."

Mom looked at me for a minute. I could tell she wanted to ask more questions, but something in my expression must have changed her mind. "Can I make you some tea?"

I nodded. While I listened to her clattering around in the kitchen, I debated the best way to tell her that I wanted to move back to San Francisco. It didn't seem like such a great idea anymore.

Five minutes later she brought me tea: sugar cookie flavor, my favorite. I sat up and sipped some, but it didn't make me feel better.

"So," I finally said. "A little girl, huh?"

"Maybe." Mom's eyes crinkled as she smiled. "We both know it can be hard to tell at first, right?"

It was silly, but that made me start crying. Mom moved quickly to sit beside me. Tucking my head into her shoulder, she said, "Oh, honey. What happened?"

So I told her about Madeline, and Nico's cousins, and the rumors. I explained how everyone had been staring at me, and how Josh might not be my friend anymore.

When I finished, Mom sat there for a minute looking thoughtful. "Maybe Madeline's right. If you ignore it, it might just go away."

"I doubt it," I said. "Nico's been telling everyone."

She cupped my chin in her hand. "I bet hardly anyone even believes that it's true."

"But it *is* true!" I wailed.

"No, it's not," she said firmly. "Anyone who knows you at all knows that you're a boy, and always have been. And pretty soon, you'll look even more like one."

"So you think I should keep lying?" I said slowly. My voice was thick with emotion; it was hard to force the words out.

"Not lying, exactly, no. I mean, we've talked about this; it's not a lie, it's private. Right?"

I nodded reluctantly. But deep down, I was thinking that at some point this had stopped being private and started to become a secret I was keeping from my friends. Was I just supposed to go through life keeping them at arm's length? Because that sounded awfully lonely.

"Okay. So maybe we should do some role-playing to prepare for the different things people might say."

When I groaned, she gave me a tight smile. "I know, it's been a while since we did that. But it never hurts to practice, right?"

When I first transitioned, Mom and I spent hours role-playing different scenarios: what to do when we ran into someone who'd known me as a girl, how to handle it when a friend called me "she" and not "he," what to say if I was teased.

We'd even prepared for something like this, soon after moving here. But that was a few years ago. I didn't think that launching into "I've got a boy brain in a girl body" would go over well with kids my age.

"I'm doomed," I muttered, picturing it.

"Listen to me," Mom said, bending down so I had to meet her eyes. "We're going to get through this. I promise it's all going to be okay."

THIRTEEN

When my alarm beeped the next morning, I turned it off and rolled over, staring at the ceiling. I'd barely slept all night. I kept envisioning worst-case scenarios every time I closed my eyes. The entire baseball team staring at me. People pointing and laughing. Getting jumped in the bathroom, my face forced into a toilet. Officially, McClane had all these antibullying rules; but that didn't mean they were followed. I'd been lucky enough to avoid being a target before, but maybe that was about to change.

From my doorway, Mom said, "Good morning, sweetheart."

"I don't feel good," I muttered, turning to face the wall.

"I see." She came over and sat on the edge of the bed. "School must seem pretty scary today, huh?"

I didn't answer.

There was a long pause, and then she said, "I can let you stay home if you want, but honestly, that's only putting it off. Maybe you should just find out what the situation is. Otherwise, you'll be sitting here all day wondering."

I squeezed my eyes shut, hating the truth in her words. It wasn't like I could just drop off the face of the planet, even if that was tempting. "What if they all know?"

"Then they all know," she said gently. "And we'll figure out what to do next. Maybe I should go in and talk to Principal Newell."

I sat bolt upright. "What? No! That would only make things worse. Promise you won't?"

Mom sighed. "Okay. But if anything bad happens, call me immediately. Got it?"

I swallowed hard. "Got it."

She patted my back. "Better hurry, or you're going to be late."

I managed to choke down a few bites of cereal before leaving. Outside, the colors seemed too bright. It was already nearly eighty degrees, and I was sweating by the time I reached Josh's house.

To my surprise, he was standing on the sidewalk, looking impatient.

"Dude," he said. "You're gonna make us late!"

"You waited," I said, dumbfounded.

"Yeah, sorry about yesterday. I had to bring in that science project, so Mom drove me to school." He cuffed me on the shoulder. "Where were you, anyway? Didn't see you at lunch."

"I went home early. Sick."

"Yeah?" He looked concerned. "Not too sick for practice, right? Coach'll bench you if you miss it."

"I'll be there." It felt like a huge pressure had lifted. Maybe I'd just overreacted, and this wasn't as big of a deal as I'd thought.

I wanted to ask Josh if Nico had said anything, but bringing it up might raise more questions. So instead we talked about last night's Dodgers game. Or rather, Josh gave the play-by-play and I pretended to listen. We walked a lot faster than usual, making it to school as the last bell was ringing.

"See you at lunch?" he asked.

"Yeah. See you."

I went straight to homeroom, since there was no time to go to my locker. Inside, Madeline was sitting by the window. Looking up, she gave me a wide smile and tapped the desk next to hers. When I was a few feet away, she slid her purse off it and said, "I saved it for you."

"Thanks." I slid in, dropping my pack on the floor. As Mr. Peters took attendance, she leaned in and whispered, "So can you come for dinner?"

I'd been so stressed out, I'd totally forgotten to ask. "Um, yeah. I think so."

"Great." There were two high pink dots in her cheeks.

I didn't know what else to say, and she didn't seem to, either. So we sat there while Mr. Peters read off some announcements. I kept checking around, but no one seemed to be giving me funny looks.

"Finally," Mr. Peters said, "the Cardinals club baseball team is playing in the regionals a week from Saturday. We've got a lot of students on that team"—he indicated me with the sheaf of papers he was holding—"including our own Shane Woods, star pitcher. So make sure to go out and support them."

There was a smattering of applause. Madeline beamed at me, clapping louder than everyone else combined. I flushed bright red and sank lower in my chair as he went on about the next school assembly.

By lunchtime, I was starting to think that I'd made a big deal out of nothing. No one seemed to be acting weird around me, and no toilet-bowl head dunks, either. Mom sent a text asking, All good?

I wrote back, Everything's cool. Love u.

Then I got to lunch. Josh was already on our bench, halfway through a container of noodles. His mom always sent him to school with leftovers, and since she pretty much only cooked Chinese food, it always reeked. "Ugh," I teased as I sat down. "I can smell that from here."

"Yeah, yeah," he said without looking up. "You're just jealous, vegan boy."

"Almond butter and jelly," I said defensively, showing him. "So not even a little jealous."

"Trade?" he asked hopefully.

I handed him half the sandwich but shook my head when he tried to pass me the noodles. "No way, dude."

"Suit yourself." Josh covered the container and shoved it back in his bag before digging into the sandwich.

Across the basketball court, I suddenly spotted Nico talking to Dylan and some other guys from our baseball team. They kept looking over at us, but when I caught their eyes, they looked away.

The bite I was swallowing caught in my throat, and I had to gulp water to wash it down.

Josh frowned at me. "What?"

"Huh?"

"You look kind of freaked out."

"It's nothing," I muttered, putting away the rest of my lunch.

"You're not going to finish?" he asked. "What else you got?"

"Help yourself." I handed over the bag. As he

rooted through it, I kept my focus on the group.

Was Nico talking about me, or was I just being par-anoid?

"Let's use the other court," Josh said, following my gaze. "I hate playing with Nico. He's like the king of cheap fouls."

"What?" I asked blankly, distracted.

"Basketball," he said. "You know, the game we play every day?"

"Sure, right."

He got off the bench. "C'mon."

"Actually, I feel kinda sick again," I said, getting up quickly and slinging my backpack over my shoulder. I knew it was cowardly; I should've just gone over and pretended everything was cool. But if they had been talking about me . . . well, I wasn't ready to face the awkwardness. Not yet.

Josh shot me a puzzled look, then shrugged. "All right, man. Later." He trotted across the court.

I hung out in the library for the last ten minutes of lunch, trying to focus on my math homework. It was pretty empty, and I didn't recognize any of the other kids. They probably didn't play sports; maybe they were like me, avoiding everyone who was out in the yard.

Maybe these would have to become my new friends.

The rest of the day, it felt like there were more people

giving me strange looks, more whispers that stopped when I got close. A half-dozen times I was tempted to take Mom up on her offer and have her come get me. But missing baseball practice this close to regionals without a really good excuse would make Coach Tom angry, and I didn't want to risk being benched.

But I knew something was off the minute I walked into the locker room. Most of the team was already changing, and they got really quiet when they saw me.

"Hey," I said, trying not to let my nervousness show. My heart was thudding hard against my rib cage, and my stomach was churning.

A few guys muttered "Hey" back. Most avoided my eyes. Not Nico's buddy Dylan, though. "So, Woods," he said, with a big, fake smile. "We were just talking about you."

"Yeah?" I swallowed hard.

He cocked his head to the side. "Yeah. Why do you always change in the stalls?"

I shrugged. "No reason."

"No?" His smile broadened. "So do it out here then."

"Why should I?" I threw back.

Before he could answer, Josh walked in.

"What's going on?" he asked, taking in the scene.

"Dylan wants to see Shane naked," Cole said with a snort.

"I do not!" Dylan protested. His eyes darted around the room like he was looking for support. "I just think it's weird that he changes in the stalls." His eyes narrowed. "Maybe he's hiding something."

Josh gave an exaggerated sigh. "Sheesh, this again."

"What again?" I asked, my heart hammering. There was a roar in my ears, making it hard to keep up the act.

"Nico's been going around saying all this crazy stuff." Josh glared at Dylan. "Spreading rumors like a girl."

I winced involuntarily at the word *girl*. No one noticed, because Dylan had stepped forward menacingly, looking braced for a fight. Even though Josh was shorter, he stood his ground. I felt a flare of pride for my friend, sticking up for me. If he could be that brave, the least I could do was back him up.

So I stepped forward and held out an arm. "Coach'll freak if you guys fight in here."

They were still staring each other down. I got between them. "Seriously. You want to screw up regionals? He'll bench you both for sure."

Dylan's mouth twisted into a sneer as he said, "So prove it. Change out here."

"He doesn't have to prove anything," Josh said defiantly.

A few mutters of agreement. Dylan whipped his

head around. He looked seriously angry. I could tell he was hoping people would rally around him, but everyone just turned away and went back to putting on their uniforms.

Josh wore a triumphant expression as he leaned in. "Like Coach says, if you go after one of us, you go after all of us. We're all on the same team, even if you're just the *backup* pitcher."

Dylan's face was practically purple. He gave us a final glare before stomping toward the field.

A long beat passed. "Thanks, man," I said.

Josh was still staring after him. "What a loser. I wish Coach would kick him off the team."

"It's okay." My knees felt weak, but I couldn't sit down yet. I still needed to get changed, and after what had just gone down, I'd better do it out in the open. I set my bag on the bench that ran down the center of the room and slowly stripped off my shirt.

I could see a few guys surreptitiously watching. I pulled on my jersey, then unzipped my pants and dropped them to the floor.

Luckily, I'd prepared for something like this. I was wearing compression shorts, and I'd carefully arranged a sock in them. Hopefully that would pass the test.

After I was sure everyone had gotten a good look, I sat down to lace up my cleats. As people filtered out toward the field, Cole came over to me.

"What's up?" I asked without looking at him.

"Dylan's got a thing for Madeline," Cole said in a conciliatory voice. "That's why he's being such a jerk."

Suddenly, it all made sense. "Okay."

"Just thought you should know." Cole tugged at his ball cap, looking uncomfortable. "I didn't believe him."

I avoided his eyes. "What was he saying, anyway?"

"Nothing. Dumb stuff. Anyway, see you out there?"

"Yeah."

"Better hurry. Warm-ups in five."

After he left the locker room, I checked every toilet stall to make sure they were empty. Then I went into the nearest one and threw up. I knelt there for a minute, breathing hard. That had easily been the worst ten minutes of my life. *But you got through it,* I told myself. Hopefully, enough of them had been convinced.

I got up, rinsed out my mouth at the sink, and splashed my face with water. I could hear Coach Tom yelling from the field as I dried off with a paper towel. I leaned over to check myself in the mirror: my eyes were a little red, but I looked a lot calmer than I felt.

"Woods! We're waiting on you!"

"Coming, sir!" I drew a deep breath, grabbed my glove, and ran out.

FOURTEEN

At exactly six o'clock that night I stood on Madeline's front porch, staring up at her house. It was a lot fancier than I'd expected, with Greek columns and everything.

"Nice place," Mom commented.

"Yeah." I tugged at my shirt collar, wondering if I'd worn the right thing. I'd changed into a button-down shirt after practice, but still had on jeans and sneakers. Judging by the size of this place, maybe I should've worn a suit and tie.

"You look great," Mom said, leaning in.

I didn't answer. Gathering my courage, I pushed the doorbell.

"Coming!" Madeline yelled from inside.

The door was thrown open. Madeline was standing there, slightly breathless. She was still wearing the skirt and top from school today, which made me feel a little better. Her eyes widened. "Oh, hi. You must be Shane's mom! My folks want to meet you. Mom! Dad!" she called over her shoulder.

"So, Madeline," Mom said, smiling at her. "Are you and Shane in any of the same classes?"

"Just homeroom," Madeline said.

"She's in the gifted program," I muttered.

"The gifted program! Wow, that's great!" Mom said with what I thought was way too much enthusiasm.

Madeline's parents appeared behind her. Madeline's mom was tall and thin, with the same red hair and blue eyes. She was wearing a pantsuit, expensive-looking jewelry, and heels. Her dad was on the short side—about my height, actually. He was pretty dressed up, too, in khakis and an oxford shirt. They smiled politely at us.

"Hi, I'm Rebecca," Mom said, shaking their hands.

"And you must be Shane," Madeline's mom said. Her hand was cool and limp in mine; not a good grip at all.

"Hi," I said.

"Well, come on in!" Madeline's dad boomed. He had a really loud voice for such a small guy.

"Thanks so much, but I'm afraid I have plans." Mom made a big show of looking at her watch. "What time should I swing by to get him?"

I winced at *swing by*; it sounded way too casual for these people. But Madeline's mom smiled and said, "I think eight thirty would be fine, since it's not a school night."

Madeline rolled her eyes at me and mouthed, "*Eight thirty!*"

"Fantastic." Mom bent over and kissed my cheek. "Bye, sweetie. Have fun."

I mumbled, "Bye, Mom."

The inside of their house was even nicer, with super-high ceilings, lots of Oriental rugs, and the kind of furniture that obviously cost a lot of money. You could practically fit our entire home in their front hallway. I wondered why Madeline wasn't in private school, if her folks could afford a place like this.

"We're having salmon for dinner," Madeline said. "I hope that's cool."

"Sure, sounds great," I said, even though I wasn't a big fan of fish. Something about the house made me want to speak quietly. It felt like a library or a museum.

Shouting from upstairs, and the sound of running footsteps. Two redheaded kids skidded to a stop on the landing. "Boys!" Madeline's dad called out. "Stop tearing around up there. Come downstairs and meet Shane."

"My brothers," Madeline explained. "They're seven."

The twins descended slowly, eyeing me like I wasn't to be trusted. They mumbled hellos, stepping forward and shaking my hand one at a time.

"Mom, I'm going to give Shane a tour. Is that okay?"

"Of course. But don't take too long. Dinner is almost ready," her mom said.

"C'mon," Madeline said, waving for me to follow.

Terrified of breaking something, I was careful to keep my hands by my sides as she led me through room after room. Each of the kids had their own bedroom, with their own bathroom, too. It was spotlessly neat; not a single paper anywhere, unlike our house, where there was a lot of what Mom called "semi-organized clutter." It felt kind of cold and lonely, though.

Except for Madeline's room, which was an explosion of color. Pink walls, an orange carpet, and lime-green beanbag chairs. My eyes widened when I saw posters of anime characters on every wall. "You like anime?"

"Oh, I love it," she gushed. "Have you seen any of Miyazaki's movies?"

"All of them, like, a dozen times each," I said.

"Me too!" she exclaimed. "My favorite is *Spirited Away*."

"Mine is *Castle in the Sky*, but *Spirited Away* is great, too."

And from there, figuring out what to say got a lot easier. While she showed me the rest of the house, we discussed favorite scenes: the things we liked about them, and the things we'd change.

"I'm actually working on a graphic novel," I finally admitted. "Kind of a similar style, but more sci-fi."

"Right, that drawing you showed me was amazing!" she said enthusiastically. "I'd love to see more."

"Sure," I said, as my heart gave a little jolt.

We entered the dining room still chatting. There was a huge table there, big enough for twenty people. Our places were all set at one end, and everyone else was sitting down.

"Shane, why don't you sit next to Madeline," her mom said.

Obediently, I sat down. For the first few minutes, no one seemed to know what to say. I wondered if they were always this quiet, or if it was because I was there.

"Your mother seems lovely," Madeline's mom finally offered. "What does she do?"

"She's a midwife," I explained.

"Really? That's awesome!" Madeline exclaimed. "You know, I want to be a doctor."

"Neat," I said, then immediately berated myself. *Neat? Seriously?*

"Maddie's our idealist," her dad said with a warm smile. "She's going to save the world someday. But did she tell you she used to be an actress?"

"Dad!"

I shook my head. "No."

"She did commercials," he continued over her pro-
tests. "Let's see, my favorite one went something like
this. . . ." He cocked his head to the side and sang
out in a deep voice, "Oh-oh-oh, I love those rich and
creamy Or-e-os!"

I burst out laughing. Madeline let out a high-pitched
squeal and threw her napkin at her dad. Madeline's
mom and brothers were cracking up, too.

"I think I actually remember that one," I said.

"Pretty good, right?" her dad asked.

"Definitely. I bet it sold a lot of cookies."

That set her brothers off again. Madeline's mom
and dad joined in. Madeline buried her face in her
hands in mock agony.

"Guys, you promised not to embarrass me!" she
groaned.

"We're parents. That's our job," her dad said with
a wink. Which made me think that despite the fancy
house and clothes, maybe they weren't so different
from Mom after all.

After we finished dinner, Madeline asked, "Can we
watch TV?"

Her parents exchanged a glance, then her mom said,
"Of course." Madeline grabbed my hand and pulled

me into their family room, which had an enormous TV and a giant circular couch facing it. I surreptitiously checked my watch: seven thirty, which meant we still had an hour before Mom came back. "So . . . what do you want to watch?" Madeline asked, suddenly looking shy.

I shrugged. "Whatever. You choose."

"Have you seen *Steamboy*? It's really good."

I'd seen it at least three times, but I said, "Sure, sounds great."

She started the movie and plopped down on the couch. I sat a few feet away. It was actually a good thing I'd seen the movie before, because it was really hard to focus on it. I was hyper-self-conscious; it was like I'd forgotten how to just sit. I kept shifting, feeling like my legs or arms were in the wrong place. It didn't help that the couch was so soft. I kept sinking into it at weird angles.

"Is the couch eating you?" Madeline finally asked.

"A little bit," I admitted.

"It does that. I used to have another brother," she said gravely.

I gaped at her, not knowing what to say, until she burst out laughing. Then I started laughing, too.

"Wow, you really *are* a good actress," I said.

"Ugh." Madeline grimaced. "It was horrible. I hated it."

"Then why'd you do it?"

"Mom started taking me to auditions when I was a baby. She moved here to become an actress, but she didn't get much work," Madeline said matter-of-factly. "And she thought that maybe if she'd started younger, with singing and dancing lessons, it would've turned out different."

"So you sing and dance too?"

"A little." She threw me a wry smile. "When I was eight, they cast me as the younger sister on a TV show. It was going to mean dropping out of school and everything. I got so stressed out, I had constant stomachaches. Finally, three days before the show started shooting, I told them I couldn't do it."

"Wow," I said. "What'd they say?"

Madeline made a face. "Mom was super bummed, she kept calling it a once-in-a-lifetime opportunity. But Dad explained that we don't all have the same dream."

"That was cool of him," I offered.

"Oh, my parents are great," Madeline said. "Even though they don't totally get me, they're always on my side." She laughed and added, "You should see my mom's face when we go shopping. She hates all the clothes I like. But she never says anything."

"Cool," I said again, thinking about my dad. Even though he'd agreed to the testosterone, it was pretty obvious he still hoped that one day I'd wake up and want to be a girl. Most people weren't lucky enough to have both parents on their side all the time. It explained why Madeline never seemed to care what people thought about her. I wished I could feel that way.

Halfway through the movie, there was a knock at the door. Madeline's dad stuck his head in and said, "Shane's mom is here."

In the hallway, I made a point of shaking both their hands and thanking them for having me over. Her parents seemed a lot more relaxed. I said, "Bye, Madeline. See you."

"Bye." Her cheeks were flushed again, and she looked happy; she bounced a little on the balls of her feet and waved as we drove away.

FIFTEEN

"I was thinking we could check out the PFLAG meeting this afternoon," Mom said over lunch the next day.

I stopped chewing and stared at her. "Why?"

"Because of everything that's going on," Mom said. "I bet some of the kids there have dealt with the same thing."

I grunted and took another bite. PFLAG had a local support group for families with transgender kids. We used to go a lot, back when we first moved here. They split you into groups: the parents met in one room, teens in another, and everyone else basically just played in the courtyard. "I'm still in the elementary group," I said. "What am I supposed to do, hang out with a bunch of six-year-olds?"

"Actually, since you've started hormone therapy,

they said you can join the teens. There are other kids your age in there." She leaned in. "Listen, it's fine if you don't want to go, but I'd like to check in with the other parents."

She sounded tired. There were dark circles under her eyes, and they probably weren't just from staying up late to deliver babies. I wasn't sure what they talked about in the parent group, but based on the boxes of tissues, it must get pretty intense in there.

I could tell Mom would be disappointed if she had to go alone, so I said, "Sure. No practice this weekend anyway."

"Great." Mom sounded relieved as she sat back. "Be ready around two thirty."

We arrived right before the meetings started. Mom handed me a name tag after adjusting her own. "Do you want me to walk you in?"

I threw her a death glare.

"I'll take that as a no," she said. "Okay, see you after."

"Yeah, see you."

I hesitated on the threshold. There were more people inside than I'd been expecting, at least three dozen. A couple looked to be around my age, but there were older kids, too, including a few boys with beards and mustaches. I scanned the room, trying to find a familiar face. But we hadn't been here in over a year, and I didn't recognize anyone.

"Shane! Hey, Shane!" A girl across the room was waving at me.

She was really pretty, with long black hair and dark eyes. I slouched across the room; up close, she looked familiar.

She crossed her arms and said indignantly, "You don't remember me?"

"Um . . . ," I hedged.

She burst out laughing and patted an empty seat. "*Siéntate*, Shane. I am so offended, though! I mean, hello, you're the first boy I ever kissed!"

Suddenly, it clicked. "Alejandra?"

Her smile broadened. "Yup."

Alejandra was a couple of years older. She'd been a regular back when Mom and I came every month. Our group played tag the whole time, and one day she cornered me by the slide and kissed me hard on the lips. The rest of the kids teased me about it relentlessly.

"You look . . . different."

She lit up. "You think?"

"Definitely." Alejandra was a few inches taller than me now. Her hair was longer, and her face had thinned out. She was also more . . . developed.

Catching me looking at her chest, she laughed and said, "Yup, these are new too. Thanks, estrogen!"

"Um . . . congratulations?" I muttered, slumping down in the chair and secretly wishing the floor would swallow me up. I felt a sudden pang for the elementary group. Playing tag and swinging across monkey bars sounded pretty good right about now.

"Thanks." Alejandra laughed again, but not unkindly. Sizing me up, she asked, "So which grade are you in now?"

"Sixth."

"Yeah? Are you on the T yet?"

"Just started," I confessed.

She nodded her head approvingly. "You'll see. Big changes coming soon."

"I hope so," I muttered.

Alejandra's laughter was cut short by the facilitator, a guy in his early twenties who introduced himself as Terrence. He explained that he was a social worker who specialized in working with teens. "This is a safe space," he said. "Nothing you say in here will be shared with anyone, including your parents. Now, who wants to start?"

I slouched lower in my chair. I was expecting it to be like school, where no one wanted to talk in class. But to my surprise, Alejandra jumped right in. "I'm dating this new guy, and I'm wondering when to tell him."

One at a time, other people talked about their dating experiences. Most said they'd waited until they'd been with someone for a long time, until they knew they could trust them.

"Allan couldn't handle it, though," said a girl whose name tag read *Emma*. Tears coursed down her face, and her voice cracked as she went on. "He broke up with me, like, right away. Then he told everyone. Now I have to homeschool."

A couple of other people murmured in agreement, including Alejandra, and suddenly I understood why there were boxes of tissues in this room, too. The dating thing turned into a discussion of how many kids were getting taught by their parents because they'd been bullied at school.

When one of the guys mentioned the football team confronting him in the locker room before practice, I decided to speak up. "Um, something like that happened to me, too. But . . . I think I covered. I mean, I don't think anyone could tell I wasn't . . . well, you know."

The whole group was regarding me with sympathy. "So do you feel safe going back there?" Terrence asked.

"Yeah. I mean, I think so." I shrugged. "There's one guy who's probably going to keep being a jerk, but the rest are still my friends. At least, so far."

"You're lucky," Alejandra muttered.

Terrence went on about the importance of staying safe, and ways to protect ourselves. But I was only half listening, because while I'd been talking, Alejandra had reached out and taken my hand. She had really incredible nails: they were long and painted with this elaborate pattern. I couldn't stop wondering how long that had taken, and if she'd done it herself or had someone do it for her.

The rest of the hour flew by, and before I knew it Terrence was leading everyone in a final affirmation. It seemed a little goofy, but I said the words along with everyone else. Alejandra finally released my hand. As she bent over to retrieve her purse, I grabbed my backpack and got up. "See you," I said.

She smiled at me. "I'm really glad you're back, Shane. And I'm sorry about the locker room. That sucks."

"Yeah," I muttered, feeling a pang. I was still really nervous about going back there on Monday.

"Do you have a buddy yet?" she said.

"A what?" I asked, confused.

"Most of the kids buddy up with someone," Terrence explained, coming over to us. "Sometimes just having a person to call who understands can make a big difference."

"Oh," I said, shuffling my feet. "Yeah, I guess that would be cool."

Alejandra held up a bright pink cell phone. "Obviously I'm the perfect choice, since we already know each other so well." She winked, and I managed a small laugh. "So give me your number."

"Sure." I watched as she typed it into her phone with those amazing nails. A couple of other kids were exchanging numbers, too. But it felt nice that Alejandra had volunteered to be my buddy.

"Okay, I'm sending you a text," she announced, pressing the button with a flourish. Getting to her feet and straightening her skirt, she added, "If that kid gives you any more trouble, call me, okay? And don't you dare blow me off. I text, you text me back. Got it?"

"Got it," I said, which earned me another smile.

Alejandra bent quickly and brushed her lips across my cheek. "*Ciao, guapo*," she said, flicking her fingers in a wave.

I sat there for another minute after the room cleared. Mom had been right; coming here was a good idea. The past couple of years, with everyone just treating me as a boy, sometimes I'd almost forgotten about being transgender. And when I did remember, I mainly felt ashamed of it. Dylan and Nico had brought all those bad feelings rushing back.

But one of the kids had talked about feeling lucky to have been born this way, because it made us unique and special. He said he wouldn't change it if he could.

I kind of doubted I'd ever feel like that. But it was nice to know it was possible.

SIXTEEN

"Dude, check it out. Fat Spider-Man," Josh said through a mouthful of pizza.

I followed his gaze: an enormous guy was squeezed into a red-and-blue Lycra suit, tufts of beard sticking out from beneath his Spidey mask. His arms were draped around a couple of Japanese girls, who smiled stiffly as their friend snapped a picture. "Wonder if they know he's gonna charge them for that."

"They should call fat Superman for help," Josh said, jerking his head toward an equally heavy guy in a Superman costume. It was late Sunday afternoon, and we were sitting in front of a pizza place at Hollywood & Highland. The shopping center next to the Walk of Fame wasn't a great mall, but thanks to all the people in terrible costumes, it was entertaining. Today there were two SpongeBobs, a Hulk, a Pirate Jack Sparrow, and a ragged-looking Elmo. The tourists seemed happy to hand over five bucks for a photo with them, which I always thought was weird.

"Hey, you know what would be awesome?" I said. "A superhero comic where they were all totally out of shape."

"Yeah," Josh agreed. "The Legion of Horrible. And the villains could be just as bad. Like instead of Magneto, it would be Repulso."

"Nico would make a good Repulso," I said, remembering his sneer. Just thinking about him made my stomach twist, and I put down my slice. "His superpower would be how bad his breath smells."

Josh laughed. "Totally, dude. And Dylan's his sidekick, Snot."

I cracked up. Picturing the two of them in capes and masks actually made them a little less scary.

"What would your superpower be, if you could have one?"

"I don't know," I lied. It was actually something I'd known for a long time. I hesitated, then said, "Maybe the power to change into anything I wanted."

"Yeah, that would be cool." Josh nodded. "Not as cool as flying, though."

"Flying would be awesome," I agreed. Josh probably thought I meant changing into a wall of ice, or a cheetah. I wondered what he'd say if I told him the truth. Lately, I'd had so many opportunities, but every time I chickened out. Even though he was my best friend, I had no clue how he'd react, and that was terrifying. But it was getting harder and harder. If you never got to share the most important part of yourself with the people you were closest to, wasn't that basically the same as lying? Should I just tell him?

I drew a deep breath, but before I could say anything, he asked, "So how was dinner with Madeline?"

I hesitated, then said, "Fine, I guess."

Loudly slurping the last of his soda, he asked, "Did you kiss her?"

I gave him a look. "Dude, her parents were right there."

"So you just held her hand?" he ventured.

"No." I shifted in my seat.

"Man." Josh shook his head and sighed. "Guess I won't be coming to you for advice."

I flicked a straw at him. "Shut up."

Batting it away, he continued, "I'd probably be better off asking my dad."

"Probably," I agreed gravely. He laughed.

It was starting to get late, so we paid the bill, then worked our way through the crowd. We both lived two subway stops away; Mom didn't love me taking the subway, but as long as it was before six o'clock and Josh was with me, she'd given permission.

We swept our passes through the turnstile, then ran to catch a train that had just pulled into the station. We settled into seats across from each other in the nearly empty subway car. "So Madeline's friends with Naomi, right?" he said after a minute.

"Yeah, I think so. Why?" Naomi was another girl in our class.

"Just wondering." After a garbled voice announced the next stop, he continued, "Has she ever said anything about me?"

"Who, Madeline?" I asked, perplexed.

Josh made an aggravated noise. "No, Naomi."

My eyes widened; he was trying way too hard to sound nonchalant. "You like her or something?"

He shrugged, playing it cool, but his cheeks were bright red. "She's okay."

"Dude!" I laughed. "You like her!"

"Shut up," he muttered, flushing even redder.

I was tempted to make fun of him, but he'd actually been pretty great about Madeline. "Naomi's nice."

"Yeah, she is." He avoided my eyes. "Maybe you could find out what she thinks of me without, you know, asking."

"Sure, that sounds easy," I said sarcastically, rolling my eyes.

"Forget it," he grumbled.

"I'm just kidding, dude."

"No, I mean it. Forget I said anything."

He barely looked at me as we got off the train at our stop. As we climbed the stairs to street level, I said, "We're cool, right?"

"Yeah, sure." But he was still avoiding my eyes.

"Hey." I grabbed his arm, stopping him. "What's up?"

"Nothing," Josh muttered. "It's just . . . you've got a girlfriend now, and you're having dinner with her folks and stuff, and . . . I don't know. I guess I feel left out."

The streetlamps clicked on even though it was still light outside. "I'm not leaving you out."

"Yeah, right." He started walking.

My house was in the other direction, but I followed him. "Hang on, dude. Seriously, you're my best friend. That's not gonna change."

He stopped and stared at me. "Yeah, it will. You guys will be together all the time, and I'll hardly see you, and that just sucks."

"That's not going to happen," I said forcefully. "Team Shosh. Right?" I held out my fist for him to bump it.

He stared at it for a second, then grudgingly tapped it with his own. "Team Shosh."

"See you tomorrow?"

"Yeah. See you."

———————

When I got home, Mom was sitting in her reading chair in the living room, staring off into space, a book open in her lap.

"Hi, Mom."

She started, then said, "Oh, hi, honey."

She looked worn out. I went over and gave her a hug. "I love you."

She squeezed me back and said, "Love you more."

As she ruffled my hair, her phone buzzed. I glanced over at it, then asked, "Who's Chris?"

Mom got the sad look again. "Oh, just some guy."

"Some guy you're dating?" I pressed.

Mom forced a smile. "Well, he's a guy I *was* dating, briefly. But it didn't work out."

"He's still texting, though." I nodded at her phone.

"Yes." She frowned at it.

"So why didn't it work out?"

"Lots of reasons," she said with a sigh. "Let's just say that love is a lot more complicated when you get older."

"It seems pretty complicated already," I said, thinking of Josh.

Mom laughed. "You know what? You're right. It's always complicated."

"So what's the problem, then? Don't you like him?"

She bit her lip, then said, "He's great."

"So call him," I said. Dad definitely seemed a lot

happier now that he had Summer. My mom deserved that, too.

"Is that an order?" she asked jokingly.

"Yup." I kissed the top of her head. "Night, Mom."

"Good night, sweetheart."

I hovered outside the door until I heard her say something into the phone, then laugh. I smiled to myself and went to my room.

SEVENTEEN

When I showed up at Josh's house the next morning, he was pacing back and forth, looking totally ticked off.

"What's up?" I asked.

"Did you see this?" He jabbed his phone so far into my face, it took a minute for the image to pull into focus. When it did, I nearly choked.

It was my second-grade school picture. I had on a pink shirt, and my hair cascaded down in long ringlets. My name was printed underneath, and below that someone had scrawled, *Is a GIRL!!!*

"Where'd it come from?" I asked. My voice sounded strange, oddly muted, and I felt dizzy.

Josh didn't seem to notice. Throwing up both hands, he said, "It's everywhere! Nico emailed it to practically the whole school."

The whole school. Madeline and half the baseball team had woken up to this.

My knees buckled, and I sat down hard on the curb. The world was tunneling away from me again. I was breathing hard, and it felt like I was going to puke or pass out. I wanted to lie down right there and die.

Josh sat next to me, looking concerned. "Dude, relax. Anyone can tell this was Photoshopped."

"What?" I asked, perplexed.

"Please." Josh rolled his eyes. "I could throw this together in, like, five minutes. Change the shirt color in a snap," he said, snapping his fingers. "And the hair looks totally fake."

I stared at him. "Fake?"

"Yeah." He frowned. "Nico's just messing with us. He probably hopes it'll make you screw up at regionals."

I managed a nod, even though all I could think was, *But it's true.*

"I'd seriously punch the guy if it wouldn't get me thrown off the team. Hey, are you okay?"

I was about the furthest from okay that I'd ever been. I wanted to run home and lock myself in my room. "I feel kind of sick. I might go home."

"No way," Josh said, shaking his head hard. "You can't let Nico win. C'mon, we're gonna be late."

I gaped at him. *How could I possibly go to school?*

This was all anyone would be talking about. And unlike Josh, most people wouldn't assume the picture had been Photoshopped. "I don't know, Josh. I—"

He extended a hand down toward me. "I got your back. Team Shosh, right?"

I hesitated, then let him pull me up. We walked in silence. With every step forward, part of me was shrinking back. I imagined an auditorium full of classmates pointing and jeering. People throwing things, spitting on me. Madeline saying she never wanted to speak to me again.

I gnawed the inside of my cheek to keep from crying. At one point, Josh grabbed my elbow to keep me from accidentally stepping in front of a car. He didn't say anything, which almost made it worse. The whole time, all I could think was that I should tell him the truth. Here he was, still defending me, and I was keeping up the lie.

When we finally got to school, a group of kids was gathered in the yard waiting for the final bell. I could sense the weight of their stares, and the whispering was much worse today; it definitely wasn't in my head.

Josh threw the girls closest to us a withering glare, then leaned in and whispered fiercely, "Just stay cool."

Then he nudged me toward the door. I practically staggered to my locker; it felt like I'd lost control of my limbs. The hallway was packed, and everyone I passed stared at me. I kept my head down and tried to ignore them, but I caught snatches of conversation:

Nico's cousins know him. Her? What is it?

I always thought he was kind of pretty, y'know?

Oh my God, poor Madeline . . . can you imagine?

My hands were shaking so badly, it took three tries to open my locker. I threw my backpack in and grabbed the books for my first class, then slouched to homeroom, all the while thinking that being here was a huge mistake.

The buzz of conversation stopped abruptly as soon as I stepped inside. Madeline was sitting at her usual desk. She looked up as I came in. Something flickered across her face—surprise? dismay?—then she made a big show of waving me over.

I didn't really have a choice; every other seat in the room was already claimed. As I slid behind the desk, she said, "Hey."

Was she intentionally leaning away from me? "Hey. Thanks again for dinner."

"Sure." She gave me an uncertain smile.

There was an awkward silence. I lowered my voice and said, "Did you see that email Nico sent?"

A brief hesitation, then she nodded.

I didn't know what else to say. She was looking at me expectantly, as if waiting for an explanation.

"Shane Woods?"

I started at the sound of my name. Mr. Peters was standing behind his desk, looking concerned. "Yeah?"

"You're wanted in Principal Newell's office."

"Oh, okay." As I gathered up my books, a murmur spread through the classroom.

"Quiet down, please!" Mr. Peters barked, handing me a hall pass.

The hallway was empty. The oatmeal I'd had for breakfast was rising up the back of my throat. I wanted to stop in the bathroom, but there might be other kids in there.

I'd never been to the principal's office before. This had to be about the photo. Maybe lying about your birth gender was against the rules, and he was going to kick me out for breaking them. Which would be a relief if school was going to be like this from now on.

Principal Newell was seated behind his desk. He was tall and gangly, with greasy-looking black hair that didn't quite cover his bald patch. He always wore three-piece suits and a bow tie. When I came in, he said, "Please have a seat, Shane."

Turning, I froze: Nico was sitting in one of the chairs facing the desk. He threw me a sneer. I glared back at him, then stiffly sat down.

Principal Newell clasped his hands together. "Nico, I understand that you sent a picture of Shane to many of your classmates last night."

"So?" Nico said.

Principal Newell looked at him sternly. "We have zero tolerance for bullying at this school, Nico."

I straightened in my chair; apparently I wasn't in trouble. Nico was glowering at his feet as if they'd done something to offend him.

Principal Newell said, "Nico, what prompted you to email this photo?"

Nico's head snapped up. "What prompted me?"

"Yes." The principal's voice was unnervingly calm.

"What *prompted* me is that I thought Shane was a guy, and instead he turns out to be a . . . I don't even *know* what," he said defiantly. "Some sort of lesbo or something."

I stopped breathing. It wasn't just what he'd said, but the way he'd said it. I'd never heard so much hate in someone's voice before.

"Nico!" Principal Newell thundered. It was kind of shocking how swiftly and severely his voice changed. "I made it *very* clear when you came to McClane that we will *not* tolerate the kind of behavior you exhibited at previous schools."

"Hey, I'm only telling the truth. Why don't you ask *her*?"

"That's enough, Nico!" Principal Newell's face was bright red.

Nico threw himself back in his chair and crossed

his arms. He still wasn't looking at me, which was good because I felt like I'd been punched in the gut.

The shock must've shown on my face, because in a much gentler voice Principal Newell said, "I apologize, Shane. I didn't anticipate this turning so ugly."

"That's okay," I said faintly, even though Nico's words were still ringing in my ears.

"Nico, I'm calling your parents in for another talk," the principal said. Nico made an irritated noise, which earned him a sharp look. "And you're suspended."

"This is bull!" Nico said, bolting up from the chair.

"Go wait in the outer office," Principal Newell said forcefully. "And if you can't behave yourself, I'll call security. Believe me, that will not end well for you."

When he was gone, Principal Newell sat back. He seemed shaken, too. "Are you okay, Shane?"

I shifted in my chair. "Not really. What's going to happen to Nico?"

"Honestly, I can't say for certain yet." Principal Newell gave me a thin smile. "All things considered, I'd understand if you want to go home. Should I call your mother?"

I felt my chin quiver. I imagined sitting on the couch with Mom, watching dumb television and talking about anything else, anything but this. . . .

But back here, rumors would be flying, and Josh was right; hiding wasn't going to make them go away.

I'd have to face them sooner or later. I'd prefer later, to be honest, but just thinking that made me feel like a coward. "I want to go to class."

"You're sure?" He examined me closely.

"Yeah."

"All right. I'll make sure your teacher knows you were with me."

When I was at the door, Principal Newell said, "Shane?"

I turned back. "Yes?"

He had that uncertain look again. "Just so you know, there are a lot of laws in place to protect your privacy. And if there's anything I can do, please don't hesitate to ask."

I managed a nod.

It was halfway through first period, which meant I'd missed the math quiz and would have to make it up later. If I ever came back, that is, because my courage was waning with every step I took. I kept hearing all the awful things Nico had said, seeing the way he looked at me as if I was something disgusting and inhuman. The thought of going to school here every day was suddenly unbearable. Even if Nico was expelled, the rumors were out there. No one would ever look at me the same way again.

The halls were still empty. I slumped against the

nearest locker and swiped a hand across my face. I'd never felt so defeated.

My phone buzzed with a text. I pulled it out: Alejandra.

OMG moms trying to teach algebra she's getting it all wrong LMAO!!!

I squeezed my eyes shut and held the phone to my forehead. I'd really been hoping Madeline had sent a text, even though she was in the middle of English class.

It buzzed again: Remember the rules, guapo, rite me!

I hesitated, then wrote, Things r really really bad @ school.

Bad how? R U Ok?

This guy emailed a pic of me as a girl 2 every1.

A long beat, then she wrote: Oh no Shane that is awful. I m so sorry, just remember u have people on your side and hes just a jealous jerk. You want me 2 make him regret it just lmk.

Despite the circumstances, that made me smile. Thanx.

K. TTYL.

She sent a GIF of a guy in a bear suit doing cartwheels. It was ridiculous and funny and oddly made me feel better. I drew a deep breath, squared my shoulders, then went into class.

EIGHTEEN

"This week is all about focus," Coach said, rolling back and forth on the balls of his feet as he addressed us.

We were hunkered down in the locker room after practice. Coach had worked us hard, with tons of drills. After being stared at all day, it had been a relief to just shut off my brain and focus on the game.

"It doesn't matter if we win or lose, as long as you guys play your hearts out on the field," he continued.

The murmur of acknowledgment was noticeably subdued. The other guys on the team kept scrutinizing me, looking away when I met their eyes. No one had said anything, but they were definitely keeping their distance.

All except Josh, who'd practically been glued to my side.

Coach cleared his throat, then said, "Principal Newell told me about some sort of nonsense with a player from the Mustangs. Now, I haven't heard all the details yet." His eyes lit on me, and his scowl deepened. "But I'll say this. We are a team. We stand together, and we protect each other. And if any of you disagree, you can sit on the bench this weekend."

Coach scoured the room with his eyes, as if daring someone to take him up on it. I shrunk down farther in my seat.

"Dylan? You got something to say?" Coach Tom growled.

I glanced over. Dylan's legs were jiggling, and his jaw was tight. Coach stared him down. Finally, he shook his head.

"Good, because I don't have time for players who don't put the team first. How about the rest of you?"

The other guys were glancing at each other. A few nodded.

"Sorry, couldn't hear you," Coach said, holding a hand up to his ear. "Are you a team or not?"

"We're a team." More voices this time.

It wasn't said with as much enthusiasm as he was probably hoping for, but Coach nodded anyway and said, "Go home and rest up. More drills tomorrow."

There were a few scattered groans, then everyone started gathering up their bags. I could still feel the stares as I slowly zipped mine. Grown-ups just didn't get it. They could talk all they wanted about not tolerating bullying, but that wouldn't make it stop.

A hand clamped down on my shoulder. "Shane?"

Coach Tom was staring down at me. "Yes, sir?"

"Hang back a sec, will you?"

Reluctantly, I waved Josh on. He mimicked texting, and I nodded.

Coach waited until everyone had cleared out, then motioned for me to sit. He put a foot up on the bench and leaned over. "So. I understand Nico Palmer has been running his mouth."

"Yes, sir," I muttered.

He studied me, making me squirm. I wasn't sure what was worse: all the kids whispering behind my back, or the well-meaning adults who didn't know what to say. "You ever see Mo'ne Davis play?"

I nodded. "Yes, sir." Mo'ne Davis was a girl who had totally dominated the Little League World Series a few years ago. I'd actually studied her form on throwing curveballs, which were easily my weakest pitch.

"How about Jackie Mitchell? Ever heard of her?"

"No, sir."

"Well, that's a shame." Coach Tom adjusted his ball cap and continued, "Lefty pitcher back in the thirties. She struck out Babe Ruth in an exhibition game. Gehrig, too."

My heart was hammering in my chest again. *What was his point?* "I'm not a girl," I blurted out.

Coach squinted at me, then nodded. "Okay."

"I'm not, I'm just . . ." I struggled to find the words to explain.

He held up a hand. "I don't need you to tell me anything personal. Can't let you, actually. Got a whole lecture about it from Newell."

"But sir—"

"I'm just saying, you're one of the best players I've ever seen. And if this is why you've been off your game, I'm here to help you get back on it. Doesn't matter to me if you're a girl or a boy or, heck, a kangaroo. Long as you keep throwing the ball the way you do, we got a real shot at winning this thing. You hear me?"

I nodded, even though all I could think was, *A kangaroo?*

"Great." He straightened and clapped his hands together. "See you tomorrow."

The drive home with Mom was rough. She was really upset about Nico emailing the picture and wanted to call Principal Newell and demand that he be expelled. She threatened to call Nico's parents and his aunt and uncle in San Francisco, too.

Her ranting just made me feel worse. I slumped

down in the car seat and picked at a hangnail.

"Shane?" Mom finally asked, looking over as we waited for a light to turn green. "Are you okay?"

I shook my head. "No."

Her nostrils flared, and her fingers went white on the steering wheel. "That little cretin. I swear, if I—"

"Mom, stop. This isn't helping." As we pulled into our driveway, I started to cry.

Mom unbuckled her seat belt and slid across to wrap her arms around me. My shoulders shook, tears and snot streamed down my face. The whole day ran on a loop in my mind: seeing the picture on Josh's phone, all the stares and whispers, Nico's hateful words, the talk with Coach. It hadn't really hit me until now that this was it: nothing would ever be the same again. There was no safe place for me anymore.

The absolute worst thing about sobbing like this was that it made me feel like a girl. Not that boys can't cry, but the way life *should* be and the way it actually *was* were two different things. And in that world, a crying boy was still not okay.

We sat there for a long time. It was like Mom and me had entered our own little bubble, and nothing else could penetrate it. I wished we could just stay in the car forever.

Eventually, my sobs diminished. I wiped my nose

with the back of my hand. Mom dug a tissue out of the glove compartment, and I did my best to clean up with it. "Better?" she asked.

"A little."

"Good."

As we were walking in the front door, my cell phone rang. I wasn't really in the mood to talk to anyone, but it was Alejandra.

"Hello?" I said, picking up.

"Hey, *guapo*." She was somewhere loud, with lots of chatter in the background. "How are you?"

"I'm okay," I said, walking to my bedroom.

"Yeah? Because you definitely do not sound okay. *¡Cállate!*" she shouted. I winced and held the phone away from my ear as she let loose with a long tirade in Spanish. It was marginally quieter when she got back on and said, "Sheesh, you don't know what I have to deal with. Too many people in this house."

"That's your house?" I asked as I flopped down on my bed. I would've guessed a restaurant, or a train station.

"Oh, yeah. I've got three brothers and sisters, and right now my aunt is staying with us. It's crazy loud. Hang on." The sound of a door slamming, and the background noise faded considerably. "Okay. So someone emailed a picture of you?"

"Yeah. His cousins go to my old school. They

must've showed him their yearbook. He sent it to pretty much the whole school." The lead ball in my gut expanded, as if saying it out loud made it more real. "I don't know why he did it. I struck him out in a few games, so maybe he's getting me back for that. . . ."

"Or maybe he's just a jerk." A pause, then Alejandra said, "You know, almost the exact identical thing happened to me."

"Is that why you're homeschooled?" I asked.

"Yeah. It was just too hard to go back, you know?"

"I totally know," I said. The thought of school tomorrow made my stomach cramp painfully.

"Hey, do you want me to come over?"

"Here?" I asked, startled.

"Or somewhere else. I'm starving. Meet me at Oki-Dog?"

Oki-Dog was a hot dog stand pretty close to where we lived, definitely walking distance. "I don't know if I can," I said, checking the clock. It was nearly six, and I hadn't even thought about homework yet. Although that was pretty much the last thing I was in the mood for. I wasn't exactly hungry, either.

"Well, text if you can come, okay?"

"Yeah, sure. I'll try."

"Good. And Shane?"

"Yeah?"

"Don't let the haters get you down."

She hung up. I checked my phone. There were a couple of texts from Josh, the usual stuff: baseball stats, links to weird things he'd found online. Nothing from Madeline, even though I'd sent a text after lunch asking, Hey, whats up?

But she'd saved me a seat in homeroom; that meant something, right? Unless she'd changed her mind about me later.

I pressed the phone to my forehead and squeezed my eyes shut. The urge to run away was stronger than ever. I opened the door to my room and called out, "Hey, Mom? Can I go grab dinner with a friend?"

NINETEEN

I got to Oki-Dog about twenty minutes later. It was a tiny place that barely held a few mismatched tables and chairs. You ordered at the counter: hamburger, cheeseburger, or a hot dog with cheese, which was their specialty.

Aside from Alejandra, there was an older couple at another table. Alejandra jumped up and threw her arms around me, then kissed me on the cheek. "Finally!" she exclaimed. "I'm starving!"

She was wearing a miniskirt and a jean jacket. Long earrings dangled nearly to her shoulders, and she had on a lot of makeup. I could see the older couple sizing us up, trying to figure out the relationship.

"Yeah, hey," I said awkwardly. "Thanks for inviting me."

"Go order," she said, waving me toward the counter. "I already did."

I ordered an Oki-Dog and a Coke, then went back to the table and sat down.

Alejandra leaned across and grabbed my hand. "So. You've been outed." Taking in my expression, she added, "Hey, you got the first one out of the way, and that's always the worst."

"How can it happen more than once?" I asked, perplexed.

Alejandra threw me a wry smile. "Well, it's not like regular people go around announcing, 'My name is Bob, and I was born a man,' when they first meet someone, right?"

"Right," I agreed.

"So you go to college. Maybe you decide to be quiet about it. But sooner or later, people find out." A shadow passed over her face, and she lowered her voice as she added, "They always do."

"So, what? We should tell people straight out? Or do we lie to them?"

Alejandra's eyebrows shot up. "Who said anything about lying?"

"Well, I mean . . . if we don't tell them, that's kind of like lying, right?"

She shook her head, setting her earrings jangling.

"Not a lie. I mean, I knew when I was three that I was really a girl, right?"

I nodded. That was around the age that I'd figured it out, too.

She leaned in. "Plus, they've done brain scans. People like me, our brains match a 'normal' girl's brain more than a boy's. Same with you. So you are a boy," she said, pointing to me. "And I am a girl. No lying necessary."

"No one else seems to see it that way," I grumbled, slouching in my chair.

"Well, they're idiots," she said dismissively. "People are afraid of what they don't understand, and we're not exactly common."

I thought about the way Nico had looked at me, and the disgust in his voice. It seemed more like anger than fear, as if he hated the idea of people like us. I couldn't really imagine feeling that way about anyone. "Did you have a bully, too? Is that why you left school?"

Alejandra's face darkened again, and she looked away. "Basically, yeah. People can get really ugly. My mom agreed to let me transition in fifth grade. So I came back from Christmas break wearing the skirt uniform to school instead of the pants. People I thought were my friends called me names. I got beat up every day, and when I told the teachers, they said that was

God's way of punishing me."

"Seriously?" I said, dumbfounded. "How is that legal?"

She shrugged. "Catholic school. But you said your principal was cool?"

"Yeah, pretty much. Except he didn't know what to say, really."

She nodded knowingly. "People bend over backward to be nice, acting like you're all fragile or something. They don't realize it makes you feel like more of a freak."

"Totally," I said. "You should've heard my coach today. He actually compared me to a kangaroo."

"What?" Alejandra burst out laughing. "You're kidding!"

"Nope." I shook my head, unable to suppress a grin. "He said he didn't care if I was a girl, a boy, or a kangaroo."

Alejandra leaned in again. "You should show up tomorrow in a kangaroo costume!"

I laughed. "Yeah, that would be hilarious."

Our food arrived. I picked at it. "So why didn't you just switch to a different school after all that stuff happened?" Her mouth tightened, and I added hurriedly, "I mean, homeschooling sounds great, but . . . I don't know, maybe you could've just gone somewhere no one knows you."

Alejandra examined her fingernails; they were painted pink today, so bright they were practically glowing. "The thing is, the way I grew up . . . they expect certain things from boys. My mom cried for months when I told her. She and my grandmother prayed for me, tried to make me wear boy clothes . . . everything. It took so long for them to understand, and then, just when it was getting better . . ." A shadow flitted across her face. "Something really bad happened at school."

"What?"

"Nuh-uh, I don't talk about that." She shook her head vigorously. "Anyway, I was sick of fighting, you know? It was making me tired all the time, and angry. I was starting to become someone I didn't like very much."

I tried to imagine feeling this way for months, or years. I could see how it would change you. "You could come to my school," I offered. "I'll even lend you a kangaroo suit."

Alejandra fell back in her chair, laughing hard. I cracked up, too. The older couple and the guys in the kitchen gave us funny looks, but I didn't care. Making her laugh felt good.

As the giggles subsided, the pressure in my chest came back. I sighed and said, "So it doesn't really get better."

She reached for my hand. "Sure it does. The people

who care about you, that's what matters. They'll come around, just like my family did."

"But what if they don't?" I asked, picturing Josh and Madeline. Dad, too. I knew there would probably always be a part of him that wished I was different.

Alejandra shrugged again. "Maybe you lose some people. Hopefully not too many."

The idea of losing people was awful. I wasn't sure I could get through this alone. "Am I just supposed to go to school every day knowing that everyone is talking about me? That they all think I'm some kind of mutant?"

"Yeah, pretty much."

"That totally sucks," I muttered.

Her eyes softened. "I bet for you, it won't be too bad. People are used to thinking about you as a boy. Pretty soon, they'll forget there's any difference. Hey, can I finish yours?"

I nodded and pushed my hot dog toward her. She polished it off in a few bites, then said, "Anyway, enough with the depressing stuff. Let's talk about something else."

"Like what?"

"I don't know," she said, sipping her Coke. "Something normal people talk about. What's your favorite movie?"

"Definitely *Serenity*," I said.

"*Serenity*?" She furrowed her forehead. "What's that?"

"It's about this crew on a spaceship. Kind of a Western sci-fi movie."

"Like Star Wars?"

"Sort of, but better."

"Are there Ewoks? I like Ewoks, they're hella cute."

"Ewoks are the worst!" I groaned. "Man, you really are a girl."

Alejandra laughed again. "I like you, Shane. You're funny."

"Thanks," I muttered, embarrassed. "I like you, too."

"Don't say that too loud," she teased. "You know I have a boyfriend, right?"

"Yeah, well, I have a girlfriend," I retorted.

"Really?" She raised an eyebrow.

"Well, I think I do, at least," I said, feeling a fresh wave of sadness. "She didn't text me today."

Alejandra's face got serious again. "If she breaks up with you, she's so not worth it."

"I guess," I mumbled.

"Trust me. And if you need to talk, just call. Anytime, day or night. Okay?"

A rush of gratitude nearly brought tears to my eyes again. Maybe she was right and this wasn't the end of the world. She'd survived it, which meant I could, too.

"Okay," I said. The tightness in my throat made it hard to talk. "And thanks for . . . well, you know."

"Sure." She winked at me. "The best part is you've got me now, okay? And I'm worth two or three friends, easy." Alejandra pushed back her chair and stood. "Now be a gentleman and walk me to the bus stop."

TWENTy

School the next day was pretty awful, even worse than I'd imagined. Madeline missed homeroom; maybe she was sick, which would at least partly explain why she wasn't answering my texts. I checked between every class, but nothing.

The only bright spot was the texts from Alejandra. She sent one an hour, always funny GIFs or links to dumb stuff, like a video of a hedgehog and a dog swimming together. Every time one popped up it felt like she was squeezing my hand again, telling me everything would be okay. I don't know if I could've gotten through the day without them.

Josh was great, too. He walked me to every class, even the ones we didn't share. He didn't say anything about it, and neither did I, but it was like we were creating our own force field. No one came within three feet of us; in class, people shifted their desks away from me. The whispering and staring seemed worse, and it wasn't just coming from sixth graders anymore. Seventh and eighth graders were doing it, too. At recess, no one joined us on the basketball court. Josh insisted we play a game of horse anyway, but that only made it more embarrassing, since I was so self-conscious, I kept missing the basket.

We were on our way to last period when Bobby Campbell, an eighth grader I'd never talked to before, blocked our path. Taller than us, with a mop of bleached-blond hair covering one eye, he thrust a flyer at me.

"What's that?" Josh asked, leaning in to squint at it.

"We meet every Thursday in the auditorium, if you're interested," he said, only looking at me.

"Meet about what?" I asked, skimming the flyer. My relief at having another person speak to me quickly dissipated; the flyer had a big rainbow across the top, with *Gay-Straight Alliance* below it. In smaller words, it read, *The McClane Junior High GSA works to build bridges and create a safe school environment for everyone.*

"We don't have any trans kids, but there are a few who are gender questioning," Bobby explained.

Josh ripped the flyer out of my hand and snarled, "He doesn't need that."

The anger in his voice surprised me; Bobby looked taken aback. "Hey, I'm just trying to help. Lots of straight kids come, too. It's supposed to be an *alliance*."

Josh looked like he was about to explode; there was practically steam coming out of his ears. Before he could open his mouth, I warned, "Hey, be cool."

"It's a good support group." Bobby looked flustered, and his face had gone red. Gesturing to the packs of kids who were openly staring at us, he added, "It might help you deal with all this."

"Thanks," I said, gingerly taking the flyer from Josh and jamming it in my back pocket; I could practically feel it glowing there.

"No problem," Bobby muttered, then walked away without a backward glance.

"You're kidding, right?" Josh said.

I shrugged, thinking about how helpful the PFLAG group had been last weekend. I hadn't known there was anything like this at school. And really, it wasn't like I could become more of an outcast. Meeting other people who were dealing with similar stuff actually sounded pretty good. "Maybe we should check it out."

Josh glowered at me. "Don't you get how much worse that'd make things? Go to this group, and you might as well wear a big neon sign saying that Nico was telling the truth. You need to prove he was lying."

I didn't answer.

"Dude, seriously." He grabbed my arm to stop me from going into the classroom. "Enough of this. You gotta fight back."

"Fight back how?" I hadn't meant to raise my voice, but it came out loud anyway. The kids in the classroom all looked up, regarding us avidly.

"I don't know." Josh ran a hand through his hair, making it stick up in tufts. "But I'll think of something."

A couple of boys walked past. One of them said loudly, "Hey, does it make you gay if you like a lesbo?"

Josh spun on him. "Watch yourself, Lopez."

"Or what? You'll kiss me?" He and his friend high-fived and kept going, laughing all the way down the hall.

I put an arm out to keep Josh from charging after them. "Leave it."

"If they mess with you, they're messing with me, too," he said, glaring after them.

I swallowed hard. The stares and whispers sucked, but Alejandra was right. It was kind of shocking how quickly I'd gotten used to being a pariah.

But I'd dragged Josh into this situation with me. And the longer it went on, the harder it became to tell him the truth. I was pretty sure that if I came clean now, he'd never forgive me.

"Thanks, man," I said.

"For what?"

"For hanging with me."

He gave me a funny look. "What else would I do? You're my best friend."

"Yeah, well—thanks anyway."

"Sure. See you at practice." He jabbed his fist in the air and said, "Team Shosh!" Then he trotted down the hall to his classroom.

A few people moved to seats farther away when I sat down in English class. I ignored them. We had another two minutes until the bell rang, so I pulled out my sketchbook and started drawing.

"Freak."

My head shot up—I couldn't tell who'd said it. No one was looking at me. I'd definitely heard it, though. Clearly everyone else had, too; there was a weird tension in the room.

I bent over the drawing and tried to tune everything else out. Something hit the back of my head, and people in the rows behind me snickered. I touched the spot, and my hand came away gooey with a wad of gum. Tears welled up in my eyes again, but I bit the inside of my cheek hard to keep from crying. Slowly and deliberately I tore a clean sheet of paper, scraped off the gum with it, and balled it up. Then I tossed it over my shoulder like it was nothing.

"Shane Woods!" Mr. Hufstader boomed from the

doorway. "This classroom is not your personal trash can. Pick that up *immediately* and place it in the proper receptacle."

The whole class tittered. Flushing bright red, I got to my feet and scanned for the paper: it had landed in front of Dylan. As I bent to pick it up, I met his eyes; but he looked through me, like I wasn't even there. When my hand accidentally brushed against his sneaker, he shifted his foot away.

We'd never really been friends; Dylan hated being my backup pitcher, and he was tight with Nico. But we'd been teammates for three years. You'd think that would count for something.

Completely humiliated, I shuffled to the front of the room and threw the paper in the trash can.

"Thank you, Shane," Mr. Hufstader said icily. "Now, if we're done behaving like animals, why don't we open to page seventy-two."

As I sat back down at my desk, a voice behind me hissed, "Tranny." This time, I was sure it was Dylan.

OOF!

WILLOUGHBY, DON'T LET THEM TOUCH YOU!

I'M TRAPPED!!

TWENTY-ONE

Being despised is exhausting. It made English class seem ten times longer than normal. When the last bell rang, I dragged myself to my feet.

I was nearly at the door when someone shoved me from behind, sending me crashing into a group of girls. They squealed, then flipped around and glared at me.

"Sorry," I muttered. I could hear Dylan cracking up behind me, the slap of high fives being exchanged. I hurried into the hall.

Josh was leaning against a locker, already holding his duffel for practice. Seeing my face, he asked, "What?"

"Nothing," I said. "Let's go."

Josh waited while I grabbed stuff from my locker. "What's in your hair?"

"Gum," I mumbled.

Josh's eyebrows shot up. "How'd you get gum in your hair?"

"Dylan threw it at me."

Josh's nostrils flared. "That's it. He's done."

"Let it go," I said, instantly sorry I'd told him.

"No way. We're supposed to be a team. Coach will totally lose it when he hears about—"

"We're not going to tell him," I said forcefully.

"But—"

"No," I snapped. "Just forget it."

Josh leaned against the locker next to mine and grumbled, "This sucks."

"Tell me about it."

I was slamming my locker shut when someone said, "Hey, Shane. Can I talk to you?"

I spun around at the sound of Madeline's voice. She looked nervous, playing with the straps on her backpack.

"Yeah, sure," I said.

Josh threw me a look. I gave a slight nod, and he said, "Okay. See you down there."

Madeline's face was pale, so maybe she had been sick. I said, "You weren't in homeroom today."

Without meeting my eyes, she said, "My mom drove me in late."

"Oh." Swallowing hard, I asked, "So what do you want to talk about?"

"Let's go in here." She motioned to the empty science lab.

I followed her, feeling like I was being led to my execution. Alejandra's voice echoed in my head: *You might lose some of them.* Madeline leaned against a lab table instead of sitting down. I stood across from her, my heart pounding painfully in my chest.

Madeline didn't seem to know what to say, and she was looking everywhere but at me. Friday night suddenly felt like years ago. It didn't seem possible that a person could become a stranger that quickly.

"Is it true?" she finally blurted out.

I swallowed hard. "You mean, is that a real picture of me?"

She nodded.

I hesitated, then said, "Yeah."

She bit her lip, then asked, "So were you a boy with long hair, or were you born a girl?"

No one else had asked so bluntly. Which was kind of funny, since the whole school was talking about it. I stared at her, debating how to answer. I didn't want to lie, and *It's private* clearly wasn't going to cut it. Finally, I just said, "Back then, I was living as a girl."

"Because you were born that way?" she pressed.

"Technically, yeah," I said.

Madeline breathed out hard, as if she was relieved. For a split second, I thought that meant she was okay with it, and my heart practically leaped out of my chest. But then she said, "I'm really sorry, but I don't like girls."

"But . . . I'm not a girl."

"But you kind of are," she said, cocking her head to the side. "If you were born one, right?"

I shook my head. "It's complicated. I've got a boy brain. And . . . a boy heart," I said in a lower voice. The rush of blood in my ears was making it hard to talk, but I had to try. "I was never really a girl, not where it counts."

There was a long silence. Lockers slammed in the hall outside. Kids chattered, footsteps echoed; but all that normal life seemed really far away.

"I'm sorry," Madeline finally said, her voice thick with emotion. "I want to be okay with this, I really do. But I'm just not. It's too . . ."

"Weird?" I finally offered when she didn't continue.

Looking miserable, she nodded. "Yeah. I'm sorry, Shane. I really like you."

"Not enough, I guess." I couldn't look at her anymore, couldn't be here anymore.

"Shane—"

But I was already walking away. My feet felt heavy; it took real effort to put one in front of the other. I focused on the steps: right, left, right, left. Down the hall. Two flights of stairs. Down another hall.

In books, when they talk about heartbreak, they describe your heart shattering, like it's a vase in your chest that gets hit with a mallet.

Mine didn't feel that way at all. Instead, it was like that moment when a roller coaster starts to plummet, and everything leaps into your throat, and it's hard to breathe again until you reach the bottom.

The bottom wasn't coming for me, though; it felt like I just kept dropping down, down, down. . . .

The insides of my cheeks were raw and bloody from biting on them all day to keep from crying. I was late for practice, and I didn't even care. I wanted to go home and crawl into bed.

But if I did that, Josh would be furious, and Coach might not let me play this weekend.

My phone chimed with a text: Alejandra had sent a selfie. She was standing in what was probably her bedroom, making a goofy face. Underneath, she'd written, Remember, deep down everyone is a freak.

She was trying to cheer me up, but it just seemed like confirmation of what Madeline had said. We were the freaks, and everyone hated us.

At least on the field, Dylan and the rest of the team behaved themselves. For two hours, life almost felt normal again.

At the end of practice, Josh came running up to

me. "Hey," he said. "Come to the locker room, I've set something up."

"Set up what?" I asked warily.

"Just hurry," he urged, waving me forward.

"Wait!" I called after him. My mom was already parked in the lot. "I've gotta go!"

Josh was nearly at the entrance to the locker room. Cupping his hands around his mouth, he yelled, "C'mon, it'll only take a minute! Everyone's waiting!"

Then he vanished inside.

I hesitated, torn. I really wanted to go home. But if I didn't show up, he'd look like a fool for getting everyone together. After the way he'd stuck by me, I couldn't do that to him.

He was probably going to make some sort of speech, like he did before games to get us psyched up. It might even work; Josh had a gift for getting people to listen to him.

When I stepped inside the locker room, the entire team was facing me. Most had their arms crossed, and their expressions ranged from curiosity to annoyance to disgust. Josh stood in front.

"What's this?" I asked uncertainly.

"I told you I'd come up with something," Josh said, leaning in so only I could hear him. Turning to face the rest of the team, he raised his voice. "There are a lot of rumors going around about Shane; you've all heard them, so don't pretend you haven't."

Lots of shifting eyes and shuffling feet as people avoided my gaze.

"Just so you know," Josh continued, his voice gathering strength, "Nico's lying. He's trying to get us to turn on each other, so that the Mustangs have a shot at beating us this weekend. Because he knows we're better than they are. These rumors prove they're scared. And they should be!"

I was impressed. Josh had given a lot of good locker room speeches before, but this was definitely his best. A few boys were nodding as he continued, "We're the awesomest team in our league, and everyone knows it! And we're going to regionals this weekend because of Shane's arm, and Austin's hitting, and because we have a fantastic second baseman, if I do say so myself."

A few chuckles at that. The tenor of the room had shifted; they were on Josh's side, and by association, mine. I started to relax; Josh was really doing it. I was so lucky to have him for a friend.

"So let's get this over with, once and for all." Dramatically sweeping an arm toward me, Josh said, "Shane, pull down your pants."

I blinked. "What?"

"Your pants," he said impatiently. "Just pull them down for a second to show everyone."

"No," I said, taking a step back.

He looked exasperated. "It's no big deal. Just get it over with."

My heart hammered in my chest. I had to fight the urge to turn and run. They were all staring suspiciously at me again. I stammered, "I—I don't want to."

"'Cause she's a girl," Dylan said loudly from the back of the room.

Josh whipped toward him and spat, "Shut up, Dylan!"

"Josh—" I said.

"What?" As we stared at each other, his face shifted. The sudden flash of understanding in his eyes nearly killed me.

Before I realized it, I was running. Out of the locker room, across the field, into the parking lot. I hurled myself into the car.

Mom stared at me as I panted in the passenger seat. "What is it? Did something happen?"

"Just drive, Mom. Please," I begged.

"But—"

"I need to get out of here, now!"

TWENTY-TWO

When we got home, I went straight to my room and slammed the door. Mom knocked a minute later, but I screamed at her to go away.

My phone beeped with a text: I didn't recognize the number. When I opened it, a photo of a drag queen stared out at me, followed by the word, Freak!

My hands were shaking as I shut off the phone. I wanted to throw it across the room, or crush it under my heel, but it had been an expensive Christmas present from Dad. Instead, I shoved it in the back of my closet and piled my backpack on top of it; no point doing homework, since I'd never set foot in that school again.

I lay on my bed. Even though I was staring at the ceiling, all I could see was every terrible thing that had happened: the gum, the name-calling, Madeline breaking up with me, the humiliation in the locker room. It was like watching a horror movie in my head.

I should've let Dad get me an Xbox. I desperately needed a distraction; if I kept thinking about this, I was going to go nuts.

Frustrated, I got up and grabbed my sketchbook, then brought it back to bed. I tried to draw, but nothing came out right, and suddenly the pages I'd already finished looked crude and stupid.

Every so often, Mom would knock. She'd ask if she could come in, or if I wanted something to eat, or if we could talk about it, even through the door.

Each time, I told her to leave me alone. "I'm busy!" I screamed on her fourth try.

And I was. I sat on my floor, the trash can pulled up beside me. Page by page, I tore up *Hogan Fillion Saves the World*. I started by tearing each sheet into long strips. Then I took each of those strips and ripped it sideways, again and again, until there was nothing left but a pile of confetti. After that, I scooped up the pieces and dumped them in the trash.

Doing it that way consumed a lot of time. At first I thought that halfway through I'd regret it, but it actually felt good. I loved how it sounded when I ripped the paper, and the way the long strips peeled away from each other like shedding skin. Hours and hours of work, destroyed in a fraction of the time. There was something weirdly satisfying about that.

When I brushed the last fragments of the final page into the trash can, it was nearly filled with fluffy bits of colorful paper. I wished I could light them on fire. The thought of making them vanish completely was really tempting, but Mom would freak out if she smelled smoke.

The clock read eleven thirty. I couldn't hear Mom anymore; maybe she'd gone to bed. I still wasn't hungry, but my mouth was dry. I opened the door cautiously, then tiptoed toward the kitchen.

Mom was in her chair in the living room, dead asleep. A book was held loosely in her hands, and her lips were pursed together in a worried frown.

I slipped past and grabbed a glass of water in the kitchen. I took a couple of granola bars and a banana, too, even though I doubted I'd be able to choke them down.

As I passed Mom on my way back, she shifted slightly in her sleep and murmured something unintelligible. I froze, waiting until her breathing evened out. Then I kept going, closing and locking the door.

Mom knocked first thing the next morning. With forced cheer, she said, "I made challah bread french toast for breakfast. And believe it or not there's bacon out here! Real bacon!"

"I'm not hungry," I called back.

"If you don't hurry, you'll be late for school."

"I'm never going back there!" I shouted.

A long pause, then she said, "Shane, honey, can we please talk about this?"

"No."

When bribery didn't work, she tried threats: "If you don't open this door, I'm calling your father!"

"Go ahead. He doesn't care."

"Of course he cares."

"I bet he doesn't even pick up."

She went away for a bit, then came back an hour later. My doorknob rattled. Sounding teary, Mom said, "Shane, you're really scaring me. I need you to unlock this door."

"Or what?" I demanded.

A long silence. She must've been shocked, I'd never spoken to her like that before. Which should've made me feel awful, but I didn't care. Overnight, everything had ceased to matter. I didn't feel like I needed anyone or anything. I'd sit in this room forever, and life could go on without me. If I opened the door to discover the entire world in flames, I'd just grab a bag of marshmallows.

"Shane," Mom said, her voice cracking a little. "Please open the door. I really need to see that you're okay."

I squeezed my eyes shut. "If I open it, you won't try to make me come out?"

A long beat, then she said, "Not if you don't want to."

I drew a deep breath, then unlocked the door and opened it. Mom stood on the threshold, her face tight with worry.

"See? I'm fine," I said coldly.

I probably looked awful. I was still wearing my practice uniform and hadn't brushed my teeth or showered. I hadn't slept much all night, either; I'd doze off for a while, then startle awake, remembering everything all over again.

"Thanks for opening the door, sweetheart. Can I get you something to eat?" she asked.

"I'm not hungry."

"But—"

"I had a granola bar. And a banana."

"Okay." Mom gnawed on her lip. "I called Dr. Terri. She's free today at eleven if you want to talk."

I was already shaking my head. I hadn't seen my therapist in over a year, and I wasn't about to open up to her now. "I'm not going anywhere."

"On the phone, then," she said, a pleading note in her voice. "I really think it would help to talk to someone."

"No."

Mom's face fell. I felt a twinge of guilt; she was only trying to help. But no one could make this better. "I love you, honey. Please tell me what I can do."

"You can leave me alone," I said. Then I shut and locked the door again.

Mom left lunch outside my door. She knocked and said, "There's a sandwich out here in case you change your mind."

I didn't answer, but after her footsteps faded, I opened the door and took the plate. The sandwich was almond butter, banana, and raisin, which was usually my favorite. I barely tasted it, though; it turned to paste in my mouth. I ate a few bites, then put the plate back in the hallway.

I only left to go to the bathroom, then I came right back. Each time I passed Mom, she'd try to smile at me, but I ignored her. I heard her on the phone a few times talking in a low voice, probably to Dr. Terri, or maybe Dad. But she didn't try to force me out of the room again.

I spent most of the day lying on my bed, staring at the ceiling. It was really hard not to check my phone, but every time I considered it, I saw that awful text again. Instead, I passed the time by coming up with ways to escape. I could sneak out at night. Take money from Mom's purse and get on a bus headed somewhere I'd never been. Arizona was supposed to be nice and hot; that was where a lot of baseball teams went for spring training. I bet you could sleep outside most of the year and not even get cold. Or I could go to Alaska and work on a fishing boat; there were a lot of TV shows where guys did that. They were all older, but maybe age didn't matter as long as you were willing to work hard. I wasn't sure if I'd get seasick, though, since I'd never been on anything but a ferry before.

Around dinnertime, Mom knocked again. "Shane, it's time for your shot. Dr. Anne said it's important to do it around the same time every week, so we really should've done it last night."

I sat up in bed. Had it only been eight days since my first shot? It felt like a lifetime ago.

"I could come in real quick and give it to you," Mom offered.

"What's the point?" I growled. "It's not like I'm fooling anyone."

Silence on the other side of the door. Then Mom said, "Why don't we just go ahead and do it anyway? I have it all ready."

"Fine." I rolled off the bed and stomped to the door.

Mom was standing there, holding the needle. I pulled down my sweatpants to expose my upper thigh.

"All set?" Mom asked.

I nodded. She wiped my leg with an antiseptic pad and stuck me with the needle. I winced and kept my head turned away. It was funny to think I'd been excited the first time. Like a dumb kid who thought this would change anything.

"Done," Mom announced.

I pulled my pants back up.

Hesitantly, Mom said, "I was thinking about ordering Chinese food tonight. Does that sound good?"

"Whatever." I shrugged. "I'm not hungry."

Mom was wearing sweats, too, and hairs had slipped free from her ponytail. She looked pale, and there were dark circles under her eyes. She inhaled deeply, then said, "I rented *Firefly*. It's been awhile since we watched it together."

"I'm too old for that."

"But it's your favorite show!" she exclaimed.

"Not anymore." I was already heading back to bed.

Mom peered into my overflowing trash can. "What's all this?"

"My graphic novel. It was stupid, so I got rid of it."

Mom gasped. "Oh, Shane."

Before I could reply, the doorbell rang.

"Must be the food," I muttered.

"I haven't ordered yet." Mom's brow furrowed, then suddenly her eyes widened. "Oh no."

"What?"

She was already heading for the door, pulling out her ponytail and running a hand through her hair as she went. She looked frantic.

The sound of the front door opening, then a man's voice. I snuck into the hall to listen.

"I am so sorry!" Mom was exclaiming. "We've been dealing with a bit of a family emergency here, and it totally slipped my mind."

I couldn't hear the response, his voice was too low. I crept to the living room doorway.

There was a guy standing in our foyer. He was tall, with salt-and-pepper hair worn a little long over his ears, and the kind of scruff you had to work at. He was holding a bottle of wine and looking pretty bummed out.

Glancing over Mom's shoulder, he saw me and broke into a smile. "Hey," he said, striding forward. "You must be Shane."

"Are you Chris?" I asked, automatically shaking his hand.

"The one and only."

It was a goofy answer; I almost rolled my eyes. Up close, his teeth were that fake bleached white you saw a lot of in Los Angeles. He was wearing jeans that looked old but were really new, too.

"Chris and I were supposed to have dinner tonight." Mom was wringing her hands. "I forgot to call and cancel."

"Oh," I said. Chris was checking me out, while

trying to look like he wasn't. I took a small step back, suddenly aware of how bad I must smell. "Well, don't let me stop you."

"Shane is a little . . . under the weather," Mom explained.

"Sorry, man. That's a drag," Chris said.

A drag? I thought. *Who talks like that?* "You should go, Mom. I'm fine here by myself."

Chris turned back to Mom, looking hopeful, but she was already shaking her head. "I'm so sorry, but I really can't leave him alone. Can we reschedule?"

"Sure," he said, the disappointment plain in his voice. Handing her the wine, he added, "Might as well hold on to this until then."

"Thanks, that's very sweet." Mom smiled, but her eyes were sad.

"Well, nice to meet you, Shane." He nodded at me. "Rebecca, I'll talk to you soon."

"Yes, soon," Mom said, closing the door behind him. She waited a few beats before turning back to me.

"So that was Chris," I said.

"Yes." Mom ran a hand across her forehead.

"You should've gone," I muttered. "I'm just going back to my room anyway."

"I'm not leaving you alone, honey," Mom said.

"Whatever," I said, turning back toward my room. Lying on my bed a few minutes later, I was pretty sure I heard her crying. But then the TV turned on and drowned it out.

At Mom's insistence, I sat at the kitchen table with her and choked down a few bites of Chinese food. Then I went straight back to bed.

I couldn't seem to pull out of it. I'd never felt this way before, like all the color had been sucked from the world. My favorite foods tasted awful. Everything I usually liked seemed stupid and pointless. Even my bed wasn't as comfortable as usual.

But I kept lying on it anyway. I'd memorized the swirls in the ceiling, the brown spots where water must've leaked from a pipe. I didn't sleep for more than an hour at a stretch. The rest of the time I just lay there, willing it all to go away.

Thursday morning, I got up and ate a few bites of cereal. Mom watched from across the table, a forgotten mug of tea steaming in her hands. "Would you like to take a shower? It might make you feel better."

I ran a hand over my hair; the gum was still there. It was hard now, with bits of fuzz stuck to it. It had been three days since I'd bathed, and I was pretty ripe. "I guess."

"Great!" she said.

I rinsed out my bowl and put it in the dishwasher. Then I slumped to the bathroom and shut the door.

I turned the shower on as hot as I could stand it and stood beneath the spray, eyes closed. I washed under my arms, then tilted my head back and let the soap rinse off. I couldn't bear to clean anywhere else. My body felt like a traitor. I hated everything about it. I suddenly understood why some of the kids in the support group hurt themselves; they were trying to carve off the pieces that didn't belong.

Mom's razor suddenly looked really tempting.

I swallowed hard and turned away from it. I felt weak. I could tell I'd lost weight; my ribs and collarbone were sticking out. And there was still gum in my hair. I squirted shampoo on the loofah and scrubbed away at it. Little bits came free, tangled with short strands of hair that swirled in the drain. I rubbed as hard as I could, back and forth, over and over, until the spot felt raw and tender. Then I stepped out and toweled off, avoiding the mirror.

Ten minutes later, I was back in my room wearing a clean pair of sweats. Mom knocked and came in. "Better?"

"Not really."

"Um, there's someone coming to see you."

I sat up and frowned at her. "Who?"

"Alejandra."

"Mom!" I yelled. "You called her? How did you even get her number?"

"From the group," Mom said guiltily.

"I don't want to see her." I threw myself back and stuffed the pillow over my face. "I don't want to see anyone."

"Well, I don't know what else to do." Mom sounded defeated. "You won't talk to me, or your friends."

"I don't have friends anymore."

"I'm sure that's not true." The bed creaked as she sat on the end of it. "I thought maybe she could cheer you up."

"She can't. Nothing can."

"Well, it certainly can't hurt," Mom said firmly. I heard her moving around the room. The sound of my shades being opened, and the room brightened.

"I want them closed!" I growled.

"Too bad."

I yanked the pillow off my face and glared at her. "What?"

"You heard me." Glaring back, Mom said, "If you act like a five-year-old, then I'm going to treat you like one. Now get up and put some real clothes on."

"No." I rolled to face the wall.

"Suit yourself. But she'll be here soon."

"I won't come out," I protested. "I'll lock the door again."

"Now that would just be rude," Mom snapped. "And I didn't raise a child without manners."

A wave of frustration roiled up inside me. Balling my fists, I shouted, "Stop trying to make it better. It's not going to get better. You're just making it all worse. I hate you!"

Mom sucked in a breath and put a hand to her mouth. As soon as the words left my mouth, I regretted them. I'd never said anything like that to her before, not ever.

"I'm sorry," I offered, sitting up, but it was too late. Mom was crying, her shoulders shaking with the force of it. She quickly walked out of the room.

"Mom," I said, hurrying after her. "Please, Mom. I didn't mean it. I'm really sorry. . . ."

Her door slammed shut. I was left staring at it, feeling awful.

Now I was really, truly alone.

TWENTY-THREE

I sat in the hallway outside her door, not knowing what to do. I'd never heard my mom cry like that before, gasping and sobbing. It was scary and horrible and all my fault.

After about fifteen minutes, the sobs grew further apart, then faded entirely. I heard footsteps moving across her room, then the sound of the bathroom sink turning on. When she came back out, her face was bright red and set as stone.

"Mom," I said, getting to my feet. "I didn't mean it."

"I know. Come here," she said, opening her arms wide. Relieved, I stepped into the hug and squeezed her as hard as I could.

"I love you," I said, my voice cracking. "I'm sorry."

"I love you too, sweetheart. More than anything."

She kissed the top of my head. "And I get it. You're angry, and upset. It's been a rough week."

"The worst," I muttered. "But I shouldn't have said that."

"Well, I'd definitely prefer that you didn't." She gave me a rueful smile. "I just wish there was something I could do. I guess I keep doing the wrong thing because I can't figure out what the right thing is."

"At least you're trying," I said. "That counts." I felt terrible about making her cry. She was the one person who had always been there for me, no matter what. And feeling like I'd lost her, even briefly, made me realize that the last thing I wanted was to be all alone.

Mom sighed. "I miss the days when chocolate-covered pretzels were all it took to cheer you up."

My stomach chose that moment to growl loudly. "I am pretty hungry," I admitted.

"Well, that I can fix," she said, smiling at me. "I'll run to the store."

"It doesn't have to be pretzels," I said quickly. "I mean, I can eat whatever."

"Are you kidding? I'm dying for some. I haven't had them in ages." The doorbell rang. "That must be Alejandra," Mom said. "Should I send her away?"

"That's okay," I said. "I kind of want to talk to her after all."

Alejandra was wearing a miniskirt, a black tank top, and lots of makeup. Mom's eyebrows shot up when she saw her, but all she said was, "Thanks so much for coming by. Can I get you anything?"

"Hi, Shane's mom," Alejandra said, kissing her once on each cheek.

Mom burst out laughing. "Well, if we're on kissing terms, you should probably call me Rebecca."

"Rebecca," Alejandra said. "I would love some water, if that's okay."

"Sure. Shane can show you where the cups are. I'm just running out for chocolate-covered pretzels. Can I grab you something from the store?"

Alejandra looked at us like we were crazy, but she said, "No, thank you. I'm fine."

She sounded oddly formal. As she came in, her eyes swept across the room. When they landed on me, I tugged self-consciously at my T-shirt.

"I see you got dressed for the occasion," she joked, coming over to hug me. She planted a kiss on each of my cheeks, too.

"Okay, kids. I'll be back soon," Mom said, picking up her purse and giving us a final wave.

"So." Alejandra stepped back. Putting both hands on her hips, she appraised me. "You look terrible."

"Gee, thanks," I muttered.

"Your mom said things got bad at school. Was it

that same jerk?" She leaned in and lowered her voice. "Did he hurt you?"

"No, nothing like that," I said. "But my girlfriend broke up with me. I mean, not that she was exactly my girlfriend, but she kind of was. And then my best friend—"

My voice broke. Alejandra's eyes softened. Taking my arm, she guided me to the sofa. "Okay," she said. "Tell me exactly how it went down."

So I did. She listened, nodding encouragingly every once in a while. When I got to the part about the locker room, it was really hard—almost like being there again. The whole team looking at me like I was some kind of freak. And Josh, defending me, only to have it thrown in his face.

When I finished, Alejandra stared at me for a long moment. Then she said, "That's it?"

"That's not enough?" I said, stupefied.

"Well, no, I mean . . . sure, that all sounds tough. But your mom made it sound like you were about to climb out on a ledge or something."

"I haven't gotten out of bed in two days!" I practically shouted. "I've barely eaten."

"Yeah, I get it," she said. "I just thought it might be something worse."

"What could be worse?"

"Trust me," she said darkly. "I've heard much, much worse."

"Well, sorry my bullying isn't impressive enough," I retorted, glowering at her.

"Hey, don't get mad at me," she said defensively. "I'm here to help, remember?"

"I didn't ask for your help," I snapped.

"Okay, then. I'll go." She stood up, angrily slinging her purse back over her shoulder.

When she was halfway to the door, I said, "Alejandra, wait."

She stopped, but didn't turn to face me.

"I'm sorry, okay?" I said. "Man, I can't seem to get anything right anymore. I said something awful to my mom today, too. I just . . . I feel really screwed up, you know? Worse than I've ever felt."

She turned around and raised an eyebrow. "Like you're dead inside?"

"Yeah." I nodded.

"And no one else gets it?"

"Exactly."

She came back over to me. "I get it, Shane. You're not the only person going through this. And yeah, it's horrible, and unfair. But that's life."

"That's a terrible locker room speech," I muttered after a minute.

"I'm not here to give a speech," she said, pushing my shoulder. "I'm here to give a reality check, because I like you."

"And the reality is that life sucks?"

"Not always." She sat back down and crossed her legs. "You got to take the bad with the good, you know? It's all about figuring out what your choices are, and trying to make the right ones. The ones that don't hurt people," she said pointedly.

"Like my mom."

"And like your wonderful, amazing, *gorgeous* new friend." She tossed her hair. "We're not all so lucky, you know. You and me have people who care about us, who let us be ourselves. *That's* the good."

"So how do we deal with the bad?"

"Choices, right?" She sat back and examined me. "So. What are yours?"

"Well, I can't go back to school," I muttered.

"Why not?"

"Because everyone knows."

"So?" She raised an eyebrow. "What do you think they'll do about it?"

"I don't know," I said, irritated again. "They'll probably keep talking behind my back, or worse. One kid threw gum in my hair."

"Ugh, that is disgusting." Alejandra wrinkled her nose. "That happened to my friend Sofia—she's not trans, they were just hating on her—and you know what she did?"

I shook my head.

Alejandra grinned. "She picked it out, put it in her mouth, and said, 'Thanks!'"

"No way." I made a face. "That's disgusting."

She shrugged. "Well, they stopped throwing gum."

"I could get homeschooled," I offered. "Like you."

"Yeah, the homeschooling is not so great." Straightening her skirt, she continued, "For one thing, no one gets to see how fabulous I look every day. Next year I'm going back to school."

"Really?" I was a little stunned. "The same one?"

She shook her head fervently. "No way. Hollywood High. I hear good things."

"That's cool." I looked at my hands. If Alejandra was brave enough to give it another try, that said a lot.

"They'll get bored of talking about you, I bet," she said confidently.

Just the thought of walking back through those doors was too awful to contemplate. "I could go live with my dad in San Francisco."

"Sure. But in six months, maybe this happens again." She raised both hands. "Then where do you go?"

She had a point. I couldn't just keep running from school to school, constantly waiting for another Nico to blow it for me. I'd slipped up once, and it brought my whole life tumbling down. I couldn't handle having that happen over and over again.

"I don't know," I said glumly. "What would you do?"

She regarded me thoughtfully. "I don't know either, Shane. Honestly, I never had so many choices."

"I guess that makes me lucky," I grumbled.

"Very," she said seriously.

The front door popped open, and Mom came in holding two bags of groceries. "Oh good, you're still here! Do you want to join us for lunch?"

"That depends. What are you having?" Alejandra asked.

Mom laughed. "Well, I could heat up some lentil soup, or make Tofurkey sandwiches."

Alejandra turned to me, a look of horror on her face. "She's kidding, right?"

"Unfortunately not," I said. "But the Tofurkey is actually pretty good."

"Thank you, Rebecca," Alejandra said, getting to her feet. "But I have to get home. Mom is giving me a biology quiz today."

"Well, thanks for coming over," Mom said. "We'd love to see you anytime."

"Sure." Alejandra bent to give me a peck on the cheek. In my ear, she whispered, "Remember: choices."

I nodded. "Thanks."

"And stop ignoring my texts," she said, jabbing a finger into my chest. "You know that's not allowed."

"Sorry. I haven't looked at my phone for days."

"Well, you'd best start checking it. Bye." She waggled her fingers at me and left.

Mom and I spent the rest of the day gorging on chocolate-covered pretzels and rewatching every episode of *Firefly*. It was nice to get lost in the adventures of Malcolm Reynolds and his crew; I even managed to laugh at Wash's dumb jokes. It was almost ten o'clock by the time we finished.

"I still can't believe they canceled this show," I said, resting my hands on my belly. I was feeling a little sick; turns out that eating a whole bag of chocolate pretzels was not such a great idea.

Mom sighed. "And I can't believe I've fed you so much junk today. That's going to ruin my shot at parent of the year."

"Nah," I said. "You got that locked up."

Mom beamed at me. "You think?"

"Definitely."

She kissed the top of my head. "Are you tired?"

"Yeah." It was actually hard to keep my eyes open; it felt like I could sleep for days.

"Me too." Mom stretched her arms over her head and yawned. "I'm going to get ready for bed."

I brushed my teeth and got into pajamas, then plugged in my phone. After a moment's hesitation, I turned it back on.

A slew of text messages popped up. More than a dozen from Alejandra, mostly the same sort of silly stuff she'd been sending all week. The last one was from a few hours ago; I recognized it from the Harry Potter books.

"It is our choices, Harry, that show what we truly are, far more than our abilities."

I smiled and sent back, Thx.

The others were from Josh. I was almost too scared to open them, but if I didn't, I'd lie awake all night wondering. Sighing, I clicked on his name. The thread went back to Tuesday night:

dude, wth?!

i'm really pissed at u call me.

y r u not in school?

r u ignoring me?!

ok, now i'm really mad. u suck.

That was the last one. I squeezed my eyes shut. Josh hated me. He was probably never going to speak to me again. The pretzels churned around the lead ball that had reappeared in my stomach. I wanted to write back but didn't know what to say. I finally typed, i'm sorry but couldn't bring myself to hit send.

You lose some people, I thought with a pang of despair. And it looked like Josh was one of them.

TWENTY-FOUR

When I woke up the next morning, the sun was shining through the cracks in my blinds. I opened them all the way and looked outside: it was definitely going to be hot. I leaned out, crossing my arms on the sill. I could hear a lawn mower and a dog barking. Normal life, like nothing bad had ever happened.

I sighed and went to my desk. The trash can was gone. Mom must've taken it last night. I clenched my fists, thinking back on all those hours bent over my sketchbook. It felt like I'd actually killed Hogan and Willoughby and everything else I'd imagined.

But maybe I could do something better. I dug my pencil case out of my backpack and found a blank sketch pad. Back at my desk, I started a rough outline of the cover page for a new comic.

When I was done, I sat back and held it up.

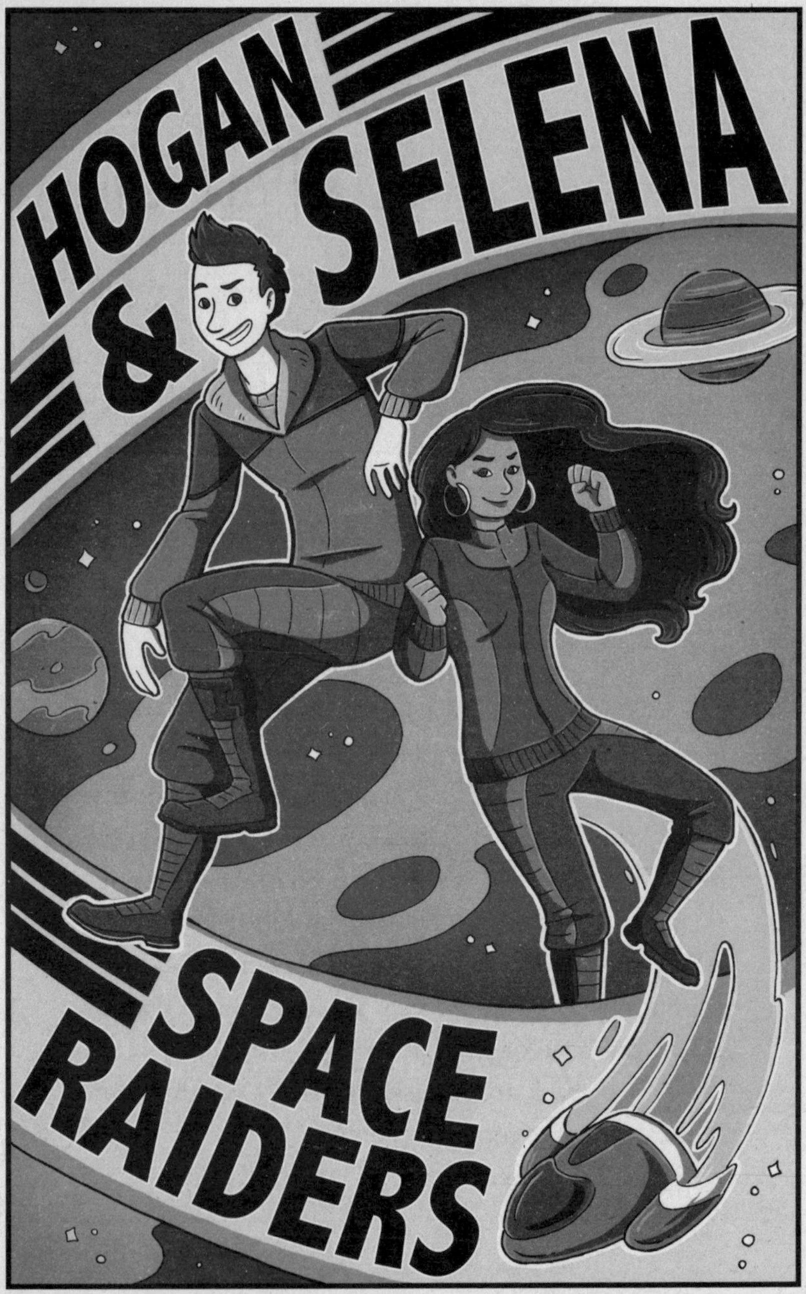
HOGAN
&
SELENA
SPACE
RAIDERS

It felt good to draw again. I was thinking I could still use a lot of my earlier ideas. Willoughby would be in it, of course, because I loved drawing him. And Selena would be the brains of the operation, so Hogan could be even funnier. They'd banter in a way that showed they liked each other, but there didn't have to be a romance. They could just be really great friends. I'd treat this more like a series, with different adventures on different planets. Instead of trying to save Earth, which was kind of depressing now that I thought about it, they'd be forging ahead into unknown territory. Each planet could be unique, like one would be entirely covered with ice, and on another, everything would be huge, so Hogan and Selena were like ants in comparison.

So many ideas came flooding in that I got really excited. I was so involved that I barely noticed when the doorbell rang.

A minute later, I heard a familiar voice. I got up and ran into the living room. Dad was standing there, peeling off a jacket. "Man, it's hot down here. Hey, kiddo!"

I threw myself into his arms. "Dad!"

"Big game tomorrow, right? Thought we'd make a weekend out of it." He gave me a hug. Over his shoulder, I saw Summer standing in the hallway, looking uncomfortable.

"You must be Summer," Mom said stiffly, reaching out to shake her hand.

"Yeah, hi!" Summer pumped Mom's hand vigorously. She was wearing crisply ironed shorts, a fancy-looking shirt under a blazer, and lots of gold necklaces. "I'm sorry we didn't call. I know this is a surprise."

"It's fine," Mom said with a thin smile.

Dad rumpled my hair. "Still in jammies, huh? Is it a school holiday or something?"

Mom and me exchanged a glance. "You didn't tell him?"

"I figured you might get angry if I called him," Mom said apologetically.

"Tell me what?" Dad asked.

"I'm not playing in the game," I said, staring at the floor.

"Why not?" Dad sounded surprised. "I thought you were their star pitcher." He examined me more closely. "Are you sick?"

"Not exactly. I, uh—" I glanced at Summer. "It's kind of private."

"Got it," she said, holding up both hands. "I'll go wait in the car."

"Oh, that's not necessary," Mom said. "Come into the kitchen for a cup of tea."

The way she said it made it clear that tea wasn't

optional; Summer's smile faltered. But she followed Mom into the kitchen.

I took Dad into my room to explain. As always, he was incapable of staying still; he moved around lifting this, poking that. At my desk, he picked up the sketchbook and said, "Hey, this is pretty good!"

"Thanks," I said, resisting the urge to take it away; he was putting his fingers on it instead of holding it by the edges.

"So, a comic book?"

"Yup."

"Cool." Dad set it down and asked, "So what's this about you not playing?"

I told him the whole story, even the part about them throwing gum at me. By the end, his hands were fists and the vein in his temple throbbed, even though I'd made it through without crying.

"I told your mother that lying was a mistake," Dad said, shaking his head.

"But if everyone knew right away, they might've been like this all along," I said defensively. "I probably never would've made any friends."

Dad sighed. "Yeah, maybe you're right. I'm sorry, kiddo." He gave me a pained look. "I hate not being able to fix things for you like I used to."

"That's okay," I mumbled, thinking it was funny that Mom had basically said the same thing.

"So are you going back to school?"

"I don't know," I said, examining my hands. "I guess."

"Because you could always come live with me and Summer," he offered. "We'd be happy to have you."

"She moved in?" I asked.

"Last week." Dad looked guilty. "I should've called to tell you about that, huh?"

"I guess we're not really good on the phone." Which was true; our Skype conversations usually only lasted a couple of minutes. He'd ask about school and baseball, I'd tell him everything was fine. I'd ask what level he'd reached on a video game, and he'd tell me. And then we'd hang up.

"Well, I want to change that." Dad reached out for me. "Come here."

I leaned into his shoulder. He smelled like after-shave and eucalyptus. I flashed back to a memory of being carried to bed, snuggled against his chest.

His offer for me to move back to San Francisco and start over in a new school was tempting. But Alejandra was right: there was no guarantee it would turn out any different. "I should stay here," I said. "Mom would miss me too much."

"Okay." A long pause, then he added, "I'll come down more."

"That would be cool." I almost said that I'd have a

giving me a hopeful look.

"What do you do there?" I asked, picturing day-long PFLAG meetings. I could handle a couple of hours a month, but two weeks straight sounded like a lot. "Is it like . . . therapy?"

"Oh, no, not at all." Summer laughed. "It's just regular camp stuff, you know, archery, canoeing, arts and crafts . . ."

"There's a family weekend this fall," Dad said. "Maybe the three of us could go check it out first."

"Or just the two of you," Summer added quickly. "I mean, I'd totally love to come, but I understand if you guys want some alone time."

"It sounds cool," I said, focusing back on my enchiladas. Summer didn't seem so bad after all. And she was going to be part of the family now, so Dad was right—we should get to know each other better. "You should come, Summer. Dad can teach you how to shoot golfers."

"That was an accident!" Dad protested.

"He shot a golfer?" Summer asked, eyes wide.

"Almost. You know how the archery range in Golden Gate Park is right next to the golf course? Well, let's just say Dad came pretty close to hitting a guy on the other side of the fence," I said with a broad grin.

"Last time we ever did archery," Dad said.

"Or golf," I added. "Pretty sure we're banned for life."

Summer laughed. Dad held up his hands and said, "In my defense, golf is a dumb sport."

"Agreed," I said, and we clinked glasses.

"I'll register us," Summer said, sounding pleased. Picking the menu back up, she added, "Now who wants churros?"

TWENTY-FIVE

I slept in the next day. For a long time I lay on my bed, rubbing the sleep out of my eyes. It was nearly ten o'clock. The Cardinals would be getting on a bus soon to drive to Irvine for regionals. Baseball had been a huge part of my life for so long; the team was one of the first places I'd ever truly felt at home. It was devastating to realize that was over now. Remembering the way they'd all looked at me, and the hurt on Josh's face . . . in some ways, losing that was even worse than not being able to play anymore.

All the Giants posters seemed to mock me. I rolled over on my side and stared at the wall.

The doorbell rang; if it was Dad and Summer, they were really early. Mom called out, "Shane! There's someone here to see you!"

Her voice sounded strained. I frowned; Alejandra,

maybe? I shuffled out of my room and stopped dead.

Josh was standing by the front door, wearing our away uniform: red shirt, white pants, and a red ball cap with a cardinal on it. He was nervously turning his glove over in his hands.

"Hey," he said.

"Hey." My hands suddenly felt awkward, so I jammed them in my pockets. "Shouldn't you be on the bus?"

"Yeah," he said, avoiding my eyes.

I could hear Mom in the kitchen. It sounded like she was intentionally clattering pots and pans. "Well, good luck," I said weakly.

"You didn't answer my texts," Josh blurted out.

I bit my lip. "Sorry. I just—I didn't know what to say."

"You could've said that," he said accusingly. "At least it would've been something."

"I didn't think you'd ever want to talk to me again," I confessed. "And I felt bad about lying to you."

"Yeah, that wasn't cool," he muttered, glaring at the glove. "You should've just told me."

We stood there for a moment. I didn't have a good answer for that, because he was right: I should've trusted him, even though it was scary. I wondered if this was the last time we'd talk to each other. Maybe from now on he'd go out of his way to avoid me, acting as if he didn't see me when we passed each other in the hall. It was a horrible thought.

"So you're a girl?" he finally asked.

"Not really. It's hard to explain." I hesitated, then said, "It's not like I've been faking all these years. The guy you know, that's me. It's like I was born with the wrong body."

"That's what my mom said," Josh said. The pots and pans had stopped banging in the other room. "That sucks."

I wasn't sure if he meant that it sucked for me, or that it sucked that I hadn't told him. Either way, it was a relief to finally have it out in the open. I might as well say everything I'd been thinking about, since it could be my last chance. Gathering myself, I said, "I never had a friend like you back in San Francisco. I mean, I had friends, but it was different. It was like they didn't get me. And you—" I stopped, trying to figure out how to explain it. "It's like you saw who I really was, and you liked that guy. And that made me like that guy, too."

Josh looked embarrassed. I didn't blame him; I was feeling pretty embarrassed, too. He shook his head. "I can't believe I never guessed. I mean, you're, like, more of a guy than I am."

I shrugged, uncomfortable. Usually this was where I'd make a joke, but under the circumstances that felt wrong. "I thought you'd hate me."

He made a face. "Why?"

"I don't know. Because it's different."

"Dude." Josh shook his head. "You're my best friend. I could never hate you."

Even though the shades were still drawn, it was like everything suddenly flooded with light. "So you're not mad?"

"Yeah, I'm mad," he snorted. "You made me look like an idiot in front of the whole team. But I guess I get it. I mean, everyone's got something, right?"

I broke into a grin. "What, like your weird toe?"

"It's not weird," he said defensively.

"Dude, it's like three times the size of your other toes." I looked significantly at his feet. "I can't believe shoes fit over that thing."

He cracked up, and I laughed with him. I might've lost baseball, and Madeline, but I hadn't lost Josh. Alejandra was right—the important people would stick by you. "You better get going. Coach'll be mad if you're late."

"Oh, right." Furrowing his brow, he pointed at my pajamas. "What about you? You're not even dressed yet."

"Dressed for what?" I asked, confused.

"The game, dummy."

I stared at him. "What're you talking about? I quit the team."

"Well, you might've quit the team," he said, marching to the door. "But the team didn't quit you."

He waved me over. I slowly followed him onto the porch.

There was a school bus parked crookedly at the curb, and the entire team was standing on my lawn in their baseball uniforms, including Coach Tom. When they saw me, they all started talking at once: "C'mon, Shane!" "Dude, what're you wearing?" "We gotta go!"

Josh raised an eyebrow and said, "So. You coming, or what?"

The regionals were being played on a college campus, in a real baseball stadium. The place was huge, and packed with people. When we first came on the field, it took awhile to find Mom, Dad, and Summer sitting together in the stands. When they saw me, they waved enthusiastically.

The first few innings, I was super nervous. It had been days since I'd thrown, so my game was seriously off. I gave up three runs in as many innings. The rest of the team shouted encouragement, though, and by the fourth inning I had my groove back.

It turned into a pitchers' duel after that: first they struck out our batters, then I struck out theirs, one after the other.

The bottom of the ninth inning was the Mustangs'

final at bat. The score was 4–3. I struck out their first two hitters. One more, and we'd win.

It felt like the entire stadium was holding its breath as Nico walked to the plate.

It had to be Nico, I thought grimly. Standing on the mound, I closed my eyes and drew a deep breath. I couldn't let him get to me. I'd managed to strike him out three times so far, even though he'd scored a run off me in the second inning.

Focus, I told myself. *You can do this.*

Opening my eyes, I bent over. Cole signaled for me to throw a fastball, but I shook my head. Behind his mask, he frowned. Cole made the sign again; I ignored him.

My fastball was good, but Nico was a heavy hitter; if he caught it just right, that could be a home run. And I wasn't about to let him have one of those.

Instead, I threw a changeup. It caught Nico off guard, and he swung too early.

Strike one.

His lip curled. Nico knocked dirt off his cleats, then wiggled his hips back and forth while making a pouty face. My grip tightened on the ball. He'd been doing stuff like this the whole game.

Easy, I told myself. *Just relax.*

I threw a fastball this time. My heart nearly stopped

when Nico's bat connected with it. The ball shot up in a high arc . . .

. . . toward the stands: foul ball. "Strike two!" the umpire announced.

I just needed one more. I pictured the team carrying me off on their shoulders, while Nico threw the bat and stomped off the field. It was a good image.

Unfortunately, it distracted me, and my next throw flew wide of the plate. "Ball one!" the umpire yelled.

"You throw like a girl!" Nico called out.

An angry murmur from the stands, and the ump said, "Watch it. Any more of that and I'll send you to the bench."

"Yes, sir," Nico said; then he turned and winked at me. My blood boiled. I wanted to run over, grab the bat, and start beating him with it.

It must've shown on my face, because Cole called a time-out and came up to the mound.

"You cool?" he asked with concern.

Past his shoulder, I saw Nico smirking at me. "Not really."

"He's an idiot," Cole said dismissively. "Don't let him get in your head."

"Okay," I said, but it must not have been very convincing, because Cole pulled up his mask.

"Listen," he said urgently. "You gotta win this. The

other guys on the team—it'll make a big difference."

"Yeah, okay," I said.

Cole pulled his mask back down, patted me on the shoulder, and trotted back to the plate.

"No pressure," I muttered to myself. Nico was tapping the edge of home plate with the bat. He made a smoochy face and batted his eyelashes at me.

That did it. I curled up and threw the ball as hard as I could.

Nico jolted back as the ball came within inches of hitting his head. The umpire reached out an arm to steady him and yelled, "Ball two!"

Nico shook his head, as if this was exactly what he'd been expecting. He raised the bat again.

I was breathing hard in and out of my nose, like a bull. I glared at Nico. He jutted his chin up, as if challenging me: *What're you going to do?*

My mouth twisted in a grimace. I wound up and threw the exact same pitch.

A loud gasp rose from the stands. Nico dove out of the way as the ball whipped past. It crashed into the fence behind home plate, jamming in the mesh.

"What the hell!" Nico shouted, brushing himself off.

Cole had straightened and pulled off his mask again. He signaled, asking if he should come back to the mound. I shook my head.

A few people were calling for the ump to kick me out of the game; they sounded really angry. Glancing over my shoulder, I saw Mom and Dad wearing identical worried expressions. Summer's face was chalk white.

Coach Tom came trotting up, even though I tried to wave him off.

"What's going on, Shane?" he demanded.

"Nothing," I insisted. "I'm fine, I swear."

"Do I need to put in Dylan?"

"No, don't!" I said forcefully.

He examined me. "You nearly took that kid's head clean off. I've never seen you throw like that."

"Just . . . please, sir," I begged. "I can do this."

He looked uncertain. I held my breath. "Okay," Coach finally said. "But watch yourself. One more like that and I pull you."

He lumbered back to the dugout. I bent over, shifting the ball in my hand. It felt cool and smooth, reassuring.

Cole, the umpire, and Nico had taken their positions back behind home plate. Nico wasn't shaking his hips now. He looked scared.

Which was perfect. That's exactly what I wanted.

I wound up again, the same way I had the past two times. The whole stadium inhaled sharply, braced for the ball to hit him.

As the ball left my hands, everything slowed down. Nico's eyes widened as it barreled toward him. The umpire took a cautionary step back.

At the last possible moment, the ball veered and smacked into Cole's glove. Nico hadn't even swung: rattled, he'd stepped out of the batter's box.

And I'd thrown the perfect curveball.

"Strike three!" the umpire shouted, jabbing a finger in the air, and the whole place exploded.

Josh reached me first. He wrapped his arms around my waist and lifted me off the ground, yelling and screaming. The rest of the team was right behind him, and they really did hoist me up. The crowd swept down from the stands and swarmed the field, all cheering and calling my name.

I bobbed on their shoulders as we did a victory lap around the field. In the stands, Mom and Dad and Summer were jumping up and down and clapping. I'd never imagined feeling so good about anything; it was like my heart had outgrown my chest, and I raised both hands in the air and tilted my head back and just let it all wash over me. It felt like winning. It felt like flying. It felt like the whole world was chanting my name.

TWENTY-SIX

"Dude, was that your plan all along?" Josh asked later, after the bus had dropped us back at the school parking lot.

"Pretty much," I said, rubbing my belly. The coach had taken us out for pizza, and the celebration continued at the restaurant and during the ride back to school. All around us, people were high-fiving and chattering excitedly about the game. Most of the guys slapped me on the back before breaking off toward their parents' waiting cars. Cole was right; they probably wouldn't have done that if we hadn't won.

"Man." Josh shook his head. "For a minute there, I really thought you'd lost it."

"That was kind of the point," I said.

Josh chuckled. "I seriously thought Nico was going to cry."

I smiled. "It was pretty awesome."

"Right?" Josh held up his fist, and I bumped it. "Hey, want to come over tomorrow? I've got the new Skylander."

"Can't. Dad's taking me to the Dodgers game, if you want to come."

"Awesome!" Josh exclaimed. "I love watching the Dodgers lose. See you tomorrow!"

"See you," I agreed.

"Rad plan!" he called back over his shoulder. "Team Shosh!"

I pumped my fist and answered, "Team Shosh!" then slowly made my way over to Mom's car. I didn't really want this day to end, and it felt like once I climbed into the passenger seat, it would. I wished there was a way to bottle up the moment so that when things got rough again, I could take a sip and remember this feeling.

"Do I get a hug from the MVP?" Mom asked, opening her arms wide.

"Mom," I grumbled. "Here? It's so embarrassing."

She grinned at me. "How about a fist bump, then?"

Obligingly, I bumped my fist against hers. The parking lot was almost cleared out. It was late afternoon. The sun was descending over the baseball field, throwing long shadows across the grass like phantom players.

"Not ready to leave yet?" Mom asked.

"Not quite," I answered. We leaned against the car.

"So how do you feel?"

I was feeling a lot of things, actually. Stoked about winning the game. Relieved that Josh was still my friend. Happy that Dad had seen me play.

And beneath that, still afraid of what school would be like on Monday.

"So?" Mom prodded.

"Hopeful," I finally said. "More than anything, that's what I feel."

EPILOGUE

"C'mon, *guapo*. Dance with me." Alejandra dragged me out of my chair.

"No way. I can't dance." I tugged at the collar of my tuxedo; it was the most uncomfortable thing I'd ever worn in my life. Alejandra said it made me look great, though, like a young James Bond. Which wasn't entirely true, but I had grown a few inches since last year and was a lot more muscular: big changes, just like she'd promised.

"Don't worry," she said. "I'll lead."

Reluctantly, I let her drag me to the dance floor. It was a beautiful night in early June. Wood panels were laid over a grassy lawn in the middle of a vineyard; regimented rows of grapevines stretched off into the distance. The band was playing a salsa song. Most of the other guests were already dancing; old people, parents and their kids. Alejandra took both of my hands when we reached the center of the dance floor. She winked, then basically started dancing around me while I awkwardly shuffled my feet.

"See? I'm terrible!" I shouted to be heard over the trumpets.

"Not great," Alejandra admitted. "But don't worry, I look amazing. No one is watching you."

I laughed; it was true, she did look pretty incredible. Alejandra was wearing a sparkly red dress and high heels; with the makeup, she looked a lot older.

"Thanks for coming," I said again.

"Are you kidding? I love weddings!"

Dad and Summer were dancing a few feet away; he caught my eye and gave me a thumbs-up. Summer looked beautiful, too, even though I'd never tell Mom that. Dad had loosened his tie and opened the top button on his tux, his hair was more tousled than usual, and he couldn't stop grinning. They both seemed really happy, which made me happy for them.

I'd been their best man. That meant I got to stand next to Dad during the ceremony, which was cool; but I also had to make a toast, which was terrifying. While everyone stared expectantly at me, I shuffled through the index cards I'd written my speech on, frantically trying to find the first one; somehow they'd gotten out of order.

Giving up on my carefully prepared toast, I finally said, "I'm really happy for my dad, and for Summer. I don't have a lot of experience with love yet"—people laughed when I said that, although I'm not sure why—"but I know that it's supposed to make you more. They say that one plus one equals two, but if you're really in love, I think it adds up to three, or maybe even four. I think the most important thing is to find someone who loves you for who you really are, to find someone who can see all those things inside you that maybe you were afraid to show people. And, um, I'm really happy my dad found that with Summer. That's all I've got to say."

I sat down abruptly, convinced I'd totally blown it. But Dad gave me a big hug, and both he and Summer were teary, so I guess it went okay.

I was a little bummed that Mom wasn't there, but she and Chris had gone camping in Joshua Tree, so they were probably having fun, too. She'd even bought my dad and Summer a present, which was really nice of her.

The song ended, and a slower one began. Alejandra immediately shifted gears, putting her hands on my shoulders.

"Ugh," I said. "Can't we take a break?"

"No way, dude," she teased, mimicking me.

Someone tapped my shoulder. "Um, can I cut in?"

Josh looked just as uncomfortable in his tux as I

felt. His face was bright red. The three of us had hung out a lot this past year, and I hadn't missed the way he lit up whenever she was around. "Sure," I said, stepping back. "I need a break anyway."

"Weak man." Alejandra rolled her eyes before wrapping her arms around Josh and twirling him away.

I watched them sway to the music. Alejandra laughed at something Josh said, throwing her head back. His neck got even redder.

I smiled to myself and went back to the table. It was funny how things worked out. My life was basically exactly the same, but totally different, too, if that made sense. Josh was still my best friend, but we didn't keep secrets from each other anymore. We were heading to baseball camp this summer for a full month; there were even going to be real pros there, including a couple of my favorite Giants players. And then I was going to the camp for transgender kids that Summer had found. Her cousin Jordan would be there, too. Who knew, maybe we'd even become friends.

Alejandra was helping out Mom after school, answering the phones at her practice a couple of days a week. She liked Hollywood High. There had been a few jerks, but she had a lot of friends, and she said it was better than being yelled at by nuns every day.

School was almost back to normal for me, too. Nico was gone, sent away to some sort of military academy.

Josh and I went to some Gay-Straight Alliance meetings, and they turned out to be pretty cool. There were still a few bullies, including Dylan, but most of the kids were okay. And like Mom says, everyone has to figure out how to deal with jerks.

Madeline started talking to me again last fall. It was still kind of awkward, and to be honest, I didn't really have feelings for her anymore. But in homeroom, we'd discuss anime movies and manga, and it was fine.

I tilted my head back to get a better view of the stars. If I squinted, it was easy to pretend that the satellite sweeping across the face of the moon was actually the *Maverick*. I pictured the panel I'd drawn yesterday, the final page of my new comic: Hogan stood at the helm, joking with Selena as they got ready to engage the warp drive. Heading out into the unknown again, their ship small against the vast sweep of the stars, their destination always just past the horizon. Never knowing what was coming around the bend.

But that's what life is like for all of us, right? Facing the strange and unfamiliar, standing strong when it's tough and scary. We just have to stick together and help each other get there. And try to have a little fun along the way.

At least, that's what I think.

AUTHOR'S NOTE

In this story, I wanted to portray the life of one particular boy and his family and friends as openly and honestly as possible. This is a work of fiction, although it's heavily grounded in the real-life experiences of several transgender children. That being said, there is no "right" way to be transgender or gender expansive, in the same way that there is no one way to be cisgender. Shane's choices when it comes to medical interventions are his own and not necessarily the ones that everyone in his situation would make. Although he feels like he was born in the "wrong" body, that's certainly not the case for every trans person. Plenty of people choose to embrace their place on the gender spectrum without taking medications or having surgical intervention. There is no right or wrong, just personal choices that every individual must make for themselves.

There are a lot of great resources available for kids like Shane, information that can provide guidance in deciding what's best for them. There are also some fantastic organizations fighting to improve the lives of transgender and gender-expansive people. I've listed some of them, although there are many others doing wonderful work for the LGBTQIA community.

For me, this is first and foremost a story of hope overcoming hate. Love overcoming fear. Trust, empathy, and understanding overcoming all the forces that are sometimes rallied against them. I firmly believe that if we embrace these beliefs, the world becomes a better place for all of us.

—M. G. Hennessey

Please visit the following websites for more information:

Gender Spectrum (www.genderspectrum.org), which hosts online support groups and conferences

Transgender Law Center (www.transgenderlawcenter.org)

PFLAG (www.pflag.org/transgender)

TransKids Purple Rainbow Foundation (www.transkidspurplerainbow.org)

TransYouth Family Allies (www.imatyfa.org)

Camp Aranu'tiq (www.camparanutiq.org)

Trans Student Educational Resources (www.transstudent.org)

The Trevor Project (www.thetrevorproject.org)

Ally Moms (www.callhimhunter.com/ally-moms)

Human Rights Campaign (www.hrc.org)

ACKNOWLEDGMENTS

I owe a tremendous debt to everyone who helped make this book possible, especially editor extraordinaire Karen Chaplin, whose tireless efforts improved every aspect of this story. Thanks also to visionary Rosemary Brosnan, PR queen Olivia Russo, art designer Erin Fitzsimmons, cover designer Erwin Madrid, frighteningly savvy copy-editors Bethany Reis and Valerie Shea, and everyone else at HarperCollins who worked so hard on *The Other Boy*.

My agent, Stephanie Kip Rostan, deserves a medal for always saying and doing the right thing, a life skill that I truly wish I'd been born with. I'm extremely fortunate to have her in my corner.

I couldn't have asked for a better partner at bringing Shane's drawings to life than Sfé R. Monster. The illustrations were exactly what I'd pictured when I was writing the book (which is especially impressive given my extremely vague descriptions of the characters and settings). I'm a huge fan of all their work, which you can see more of at www.sfemonster.com.

Finally, my family is my true secret weapon; their unconditional love and support has made me a better person. Everyone should be so lucky.

There's a saying that "You can't hate someone whose story you know." My hope is that by knowing Shane, a regular kid who loves baseball, graphic novels, and video games, we'll all err on the side of love, understanding, and compassion.

**Turn the page for a sneak peek at
M. G. Hennessey's next novel.**

ONE

QUENTIN

"Are you ready to go, Quentin?"

I shake my head. The lady's mouth pinches at the corners. Her lips are pink, too pink, and her face is brown even though she's white, which means she *does not apply proper sun protection, at least thirty SPF!* The lady's lips match her sweater, and she is wearing white pants even though it is April. *No white pants until Memorial Day—without rules, we have chaos.*

"No white pants," I say helpfully, because this is useful information for everyone to have.

"What?" She gives me a funny look. "Did you forget to pack something?"

I shake my head again.

"Okay, then. We really have to go, Quentin," Pink Lips Lady says, looking at her phone. She is always looking at her phone, even though as a grown-up she should know that is very rude, especially when other people are there. *No phones at the table especially; dinner is for nice conversation.*

Pink Lips Lady tries to take my backpack, but I hold it tightly because it is my responsibility.

She makes a face and sighs. "Do you really want to stay here, Quentin? Trust me, the next place is much nicer."

I look around. This room is not nice. It is too cold and the furniture seems dirty and I do not like it at all. None of my things are here, not my bed or my R2-D2 clock or my comforter or my desk with the matching chair. I want to go home, where *everything has a place.*

"Home," I say.

"It's a lovely home," she agrees. "Let's go there together."

She holds out her hand. I do not take it, I do not like touching, and besides you are not supposed to even talk to strangers. But when Pink Lips Lady walks toward the door, I follow her.

"This is going to be fun!" she says to her phone, but I do not think it will be fun at all.

VIC

Here's the thing almost no one knows about me: I actually work for the government. See, when I was just a kid (well, I'm technically still a kid, but you'd never guess my age. Go ahead, guess. All right, I'll tell you. I'm eleven. But I'm totally mature for my age, right? And that doesn't even count my mad ninja skillz. . . .)

Okay, so I was telling you about my super–top secret job. I mean, I shouldn't even be sharing this, obviously (top secret, right?), and it's that old "If I tell you, I have to kill you" thing, but I swear I won't kill you. I figure you can be trusted with something this important.

Anyway. When I was ten, I noticed that a black sedan was tailing me home from school every day. Of course, as soon as I realized this, I took some serious countermeasures (and, like, totally lost them). It became a kind of game for me: spot the sedan, then see how fast I could get away from it.

And it's a good thing I did, because it turns out that was actually a test. And I passed! So a few weeks later, I walked out of school and found a guy waiting for me. Now, normally I wouldn't go near some creepy guy in a suit who was lurking outside a school (Logan Street "Elementary," even though it goes through eighth grade). I was planning on shaking him, too, but then he said the magic words that got my attention.

"Victorio Quintero," he called out. When I stopped, totally shocked that he knew my name, he added, "I know where your father is."

So I went with him. I know what you're thinking: *Vic, that's nuts! Stranger danger! Even someone with a twentieth-degree black belt shouldn't go off with a crazy white dude!*

Listen, I completely get where you're coming from. But if your father had vanished on a secret mission four years ago, then someone showed up and said they knew where he was, you'd want to hear what they had to say, right?

Besides, I wasn't a total idiot. I stayed close to school, just going a little way down the block with the guy and keeping an eye on that sedan in case it came any closer.

"You know I can outrun you, right?" I said.

That made him laugh, and he said, "Vic, my boy, that's just one of the many fine qualities we've observed in you over the past few weeks." Then he pulled out a brand-new iPad and showed me all these videos. There were clips of me practicing my parkour (you know, leaping off benches and climbing buildings like Spider-Man), whipping around my nunchucks, and totally killing the obstacle course I set up in our backyard.

"What are you, some kind of creep?" I asked suspiciously (because who takes videos of a kid unless it's their own?). I was getting ready to scramble up the chain-link fence and vault over the other side in a perfectly executed maneuver when he showed me the only video that mattered: my father, in a prison cell. The image was dark and kind of greenish, like it had been taken by a night-vision camera. My dad was tied to a chair, with a blindfold over his eyes. He'd grown a shaggy beard and was a lot skinnier, but I could still tell it was him.

"Let him go!" I yelled.

"Easy, now. We're not the ones holding him prisoner," the guy said, trying to calm me down (and looking a little scared).

"Then tell me where he is!" I demanded, my hands balling into fists. Seeing my dad like that made me want to rush right out and save him.

"He's in El Salvador."

My heart totally sank when he said this. I mean, it made sense, since my dad was originally from there, and had only gone back because the country needed him. "Sometimes we have to make hard choices, son," he'd said, clapping a hand on my shoulder as a single tear slid down his cheek. "But I swear on your mother's grave, God rest her soul, I will return as soon as it's safe."

Even though I was only seven years old then, and I was bummed that he was leaving, I totally understood. My dad's a hero, and heroes have a calling.

I'd thought he'd be back by that summer, though, and now it was four whole years later. So seeing that video of him in a prison cell in El Salvador explained everything. He'd been captured! It wasn't his fault!

I started to storm away, and the guy hurried to keep up with me. "Where are you going?"

"To El Salvador," I said through gritted teeth.

"That's far away, Vic," he said. "How do you plan on getting there?"

"I'll figure it out," I said.

"I can help you."

I stopped dead. "Why would you help me?"

"Because I believe we can help each other." The guy put a hand on my shoulder and leaned in, looking into my eyes. "You're a remarkable boy with a very special skill set. A hero, just like your father. And if you devote yourself to serving this country, I'll make sure he's rescued."

"What do you want me to do?" I asked suspiciously.

That's when he told me all about this new government task force they were forming, made up of kids like me. The government finally realized that kids are practically invisible; people will say all sorts of crazy stuff around them, figuring they're harmless. So who should be doing the spying? Kids, that's who! Which is precisely why the government formed the Delta Elite Eagle Corps (we call it the DEEC), made up entirely of kids like me who are even better at stuff like fighting than most adults.

To be honest, pretending to be a normal fifth grader has been tough. I have to sit through boring classes, when I could be sparring at the DEEC center instead, learning the ancient secret art of wushu kung fu from Master Shei. But my boss (the guy from the sedan, Commander Baxter) insists that my cover is perfect: after all, who would suspect that a foster kid in LA was really a spy?

I'm getting antsy, though. I've done a whole bunch of missions now, breaking up Russian and Chinese spy rings, even totally destroying a terrorist plot and saving, like, a ton of lives. But still, according to Commander Baxter, every attempt to rescue my father has failed. It's getting to where I'm going to have to insist that next time, they take me along. Otherwise, I'll threaten to quit, and they can't afford that; I'm their best agent, the other kids even nicknamed me Ace because I'm just that good.

Hopefully, it won't come to that. I'll give them one more month, then I'm going after my dad on my own.

After all, he'd do the same for me.

NEVAEH

"Oh my God, what is he *doing*?" Jada squealed.

I turned just in time to see Vic running along a park bench. He tried to do a somersault off it, and ended up face-planting in the grass on the other side. I rolled my eyes. "Being an idiot, as usual."

"I'm okay!" Vic yelled, popping back up. The knobby knees poking out from his basketball shorts sported some new raw scrapes, but otherwise he looked fine. Thank God, because I was not in the mood for another trip to the ER.

"Be careful, loser!" I reprimanded him. "If you get hurt again, I swear you're on your own."

"Like I need your help." Vic scoffed, but he returned to the sidewalk.

"*So* embarrassing," Jada said sympathetically. "Man, and I thought my brother was bad."

"He's not my brother," I mumbled as Vic fell back in step behind us. He didn't stay there long before jumping onto the concrete wall that separated the sidewalk from the park. He held out his arms to the sides like he was walking a tightrope, mumbling his usual monologue: "Parkour means training not just your body, but your mind. Just an instant of lost focus can mean the difference between life . . . and death. . . ."

I sighed. Jada laughed and said, "It sucks that you're stuck with such annoying kids."

"Totally," I agreed. "Could be worse, though. I had this one foster brother who was always lighting fires—"

"Yeah?" Jada was tapping away at her phone again.

"Never mind," I said, annoyed. Half the time I was jealous of the kids my age with fancy phones, and the other half I was creeped out by it. It seemed to turn them into zombies. I wasn't sure I'd ever want one—not that it was even an option. I was lucky to get a new pair of jeans for Christmas last year.

"Hey, Nevaeh!" Vic always talked a little too loudly, like his volume button had been set wrong at birth. "Tell Mrs. K I might miss dinner. I've gotta go on another mission. Top secret, need-to-know only."

"Ignore him," I groaned.

"Sure," Jada said. "OMG, you should see this video Aliyah just sent, it's totally LOL. Want to hang out after you drop him off?"

I shifted my backpack to my other shoulder. "Can't. Mrs. K is working late."

"Oh, right," Jada said sympathetically. "I swear, it's like you're the mom over there."

"Tell me about it," I muttered. We called our foster mother Mrs. K because Kuznetsov was hard to pronounce. The past few months, Mrs. K's work shifts usually started before we got out of school, and ended way past our bedtime. Which meant that I was basically in charge of raising Vic and Mara.

I first moved in with Mrs. K almost a year ago, after being pulled out of one of the worst foster homes ever (and believe me, after living in seven over the past eleven years, I'm an expert). So when I walked into Mrs. K's relatively clean house in a decent neighborhood and saw a couple of sweet-looking younger kids, it was a huge relief. As a bonus, the local school was good, too; if I kept my grades up, I'd qualify for one of the best high schools in the city next year.

But that all depended on Mrs. K, and at the time, she was clearly a mess. Honestly, I was surprised that our caseworker, Ms. Judy, hadn't yanked the other kids out of the house, but that's the LA foster care system for you: they were so desperate for places to put kids, they accepted pretty much anyone as a foster parent.

Not that Mrs. K was bad; she was nice enough, and there was always food in the fridge. But she barely got out of bed for anything except work, and she kept muttering about foster kids being more trouble than they were worth now that her husband was gone.

So I set out to change her mind. It started small. I'd get up early to make breakfast and pack school lunches. That seemed to make her happy, so I offered to make dinner, too. Before I knew it, I was shuttling Vic and Mara to and from school, nagging them to do their homework, and getting them ready for bed.

I don't know any other eighth grader stuck with all that. But the more that I helped out, the less Mrs. K grumbled about quitting the foster system. She still spent most of her time in bed when she was home, but she wasn't missing work anymore, and she occasionally even made it downstairs for dinner.

As long as I kept her happy, I'd have a roof over my head until it was time for college. And after that, when I headed off to UCLA on a full scholarship, well . . . maybe Vic would pick up the slack. Regardless, he and Mara wouldn't be my problem anymore.

Although it would be a lot easier if he weren't so annoying. I frowned as Vic nearly tripped an old lady when he dodged in front of her.

"Apologize," I barked at him.

"Sorry, ma'am!" Vic yelled at her.

She muttered at him in Russian and kept toddling down the sidewalk. There were lots of Russians like Mrs. K around here—lots of other immigrants, too. Echo Park was still one of the poorer neighborhoods in LA, although it was generally pretty safe, and lately I'd seen a lot of flashier young people hanging around the new cafés and restaurants. Mrs. K was always grumbling about how they had no respect for the neighborhood. But old people always hated anything new. And as far as I was concerned, an overpriced café was a lot better than a pawnshop with steel gates and graffiti. Echo Park definitely felt a lot safer than some of the places I'd lived, and it wasn't like the neighbors were exactly neighborly anyway. Everyone pretty much kept to themselves, which was fine by me.

I grabbed Vic's arm to stop his constant motion and asked, "Did you take your meds today?"

His eyes slid to Jada and he frowned. "What, my superpower pills?"

"Yeah, those," I said, repressing a sigh.

"Nope. Ran out."

That explained why he was even more hyper than usual; without a regular dose of his medication, Vic acted like someone had just pumped him full of a candy store's worth of sugar, topped off with energy drinks. "We'll stop at the drugstore after we get Mara."

"I still don't get why she's at a different school," Vic said. "I mean, if she was at Logan, I could keep an eye on her."

"That's above my pay grade," I muttered, although I'd wondered the same. It would make my life a lot easier if we didn't have to walk an extra half mile to her bus stop, but Ms. Judy had insisted that Mara finish third grade at her current school to "lessen the negative impact on her." It was hard not to feel a little resentful about that; my other caseworkers had no problem yanking me out of schools every time my placement had changed. Ms. Judy was still too nice because she was new.

We stopped at the corner where Mara's bus pulled in every day at quarter past three. Mara barely talked, which was a big plus in my book. She also did what she was told without being asked a dozen times, which made her easier to handle than Vic. He'd become distracted in the middle of getting dressed and end up wandering the house in shorts and a single sock until I threatened to drag him to school like that.

I checked my beat-up watch: 3:10 p.m. We were right on time, despite Vic's dawdling. I leaned against a brick wall flanking a yoga studio. On the other side of the plate-glass window, a bunch of super-skinny women were contorting themselves on brightly colored mats. Yup, the neighborhood was definitely changing.

Heartwarming books by
M. G. HENNESSEY

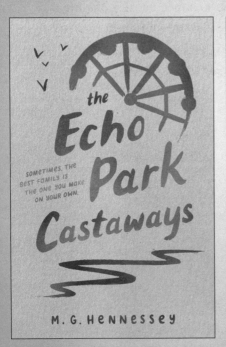

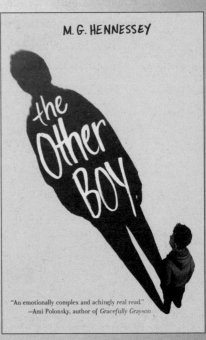